Georgia

through Earth, Fire, Air and Water

Georgia

through Earth, Fire, Air and Water

Michael Berman,
Manana Rusieshvili,
and Ketevan Kalandadze

MOON
BOOKS

Winchester, UK
Washington, USA

First published by Moon Books, 2012
Moon Books is an imprint of John Hunt Publishing Ltd., Laurel House, Station Approach,
Alresford, Hants, SO24 9JH, UK
office1@o-books.net
www.o-books.com

For distributor details and how to order please visit the 'Ordering' section on our website.

ISBN: 978 1 78099 271 6

A CIP catalogue record for this book is available from the British Library.

Design: Stuart Davies

Printed and bound by CPI Group (UK) Ltd, Croydon, CR0 4YY

We operate a distinctive and ethical publishing philosophy in all
areas of our business, from our global network of authors to
production and worldwide distribution.

CONTENTS

Introduction

Despite being located on the extreme eastern boundary of Europe, and having been frequently conquered by invading people from Asia, including Arabs, Turks, Persians, Mongols, and more recently Russians, Georgians still regard themselves very much as Europeans and it is to becoming a future member state of the EU that the majority of the people now aspire. As for the traditional folk-tales from the region, generally speaking, you will find that one of their main characteristics is that they are packed with action:

> Whilst a written, "literary" novel or short story might devote paragraphs to descriptions of people or places, these tales usually settle for an adjective or two; "a thick impassable forest", "a handsome stately man", or a formula such as "not-seen-beneath-the-sun beauty". Many of the heroes and heroines do not even have names (Hunt, 1999, p.8).

This book focuses in particular on those stories associated with the four elements, how they invariably interact with, and affect one another, and introduces some tales which have never been translated direct from Georgian into English before. M.B.

* * *

Occupying a strategically significant place in the Caucasus, Georgia has always played the function of an important bridge between Asia and Europe incorporating the features of both. This is reflected in the culture of Georgia – its customs, lifestyle, mentality and, of course, the folklore, which, as known, means 'the wisdom of people' and reflects all the stages of a person's development, starting from the lullaby first sung by other and tongue twisters learnt perhaps at home or in school, and finishing with the final burial rites. In addition to this, Georgian folklore, like the folklore of other nations, reflects the fundamental and deep-rooted attitudes of the Georgian people to the world, and the place and function of a man in the universe. Kiknadze (2008) argues convincingly that each mythological text, by definition, is of cosmogenic character and contains at least one, if not more, of the mythologemes on which narration is based. For instance, in the world mythos, the following mythologemes are singled out: (i) the mythologeme narrative of separating the earth and the sky; (ii) the mythologeme of the interrelationship between and the inseparability of the earth and the sky; (iii) the mythologeme of the middle of the earth, which is connected to the previous mythologeme (ii); (iv) the mythologeme of the eternal spring (paradise); (v) the mythologeme of the final return of the hero to their native country; (vi) the mythologeme of the rebirth of the hero; (vii) the mythologeme of the dragon.

In Georgian mythology the inseparable connection between the earth and the sky is symbolized by the axis of the universe which appears as a huge mountain, tree, ladder, chain or any other vertical object which can link the earth and the sky. It is also argued that for the Georgian mythos one of the primary mythologemes is the battle between chaos and cosmos, which is transformed into the opposition between the dragon (water) and the ox (the earth). As well as this, the ox can be looked on as the master of the earth and the most important animal in the life of a Georgian as a farmer (compare the etymology of the word 'Georgia').

This book is about the Georgian mythos, with particular emphasis on the four main elements of the cosmos – the earth, fire, air, and water. Though for the sake of the overall plan of the book, the material has been organized into four main sections, the way in which the elements interact will of course be considered too, as they are in this poem:

I also was St. George
I also was St. Georgi,
Attached to the sky by a gold chain,
Bermukha, an old oak, was rooted in the earth
And I climbed it by a ladder
And thus I took
The gifts and sacrifices from my countrymen
To our God.

- Anonymous (translated by Manana Rusieshvili)

* * *

As one of the features of this collection is the fact that a number of the stories have been translated direct from Georgian into English for the very first time, rather than through Russian which has been the case in the past, we thought it might be of interest at this point to include some information on the Georgian Alphabet and the history of the Georgian language.

Georgian belongs to a group of languages spoken in the Caucasus region which does not contain members of any language families spoken elsewhere in the world. Caucasian languages, spoken by some nine million people, are divided into three subgroups: the South Caucasian, or Kartvelian family to which Georgian belongs; the Northwest Caucasian, or Abkhaz-Adyghe languages; and the Northeast Caucasian, or Nakh-Dagestanian languages. In spite of their great diversity, most Caucasian languages have in common large consonant inventories; in some languages the number of consonants distinguished approaches 80. Those Caucasian languages with standard written forms employ the Cyrillic alphabet, with the prominent exception of Georgian.

The Georgian alphabet is the writing system used in Georgian and other Kartvelian languages (Svanian and Mingrelian).

The word meaning "alphabet," Georgian ანბანი, is derived from the first letters of the first two letters of each of the three Georgian alphabets. The three alphabets look very dissimilar to one another but share the same alphabetic order and letter names. The alphabets may be seen mixed to some extent, though in Georgian there is normally no distinction between upper and lower case in any of the alphabets.

Writing of the Georgian language has progressed through three forms, known by their Georgian names: *Asomtavruli*, *Nuskhuri*, and *Mkhedruli*. They have always been distinct alphabets, even though they have been used together to write the same languages, and even though these alphabets share the same letter names. Although the most recent alphabet, *Mkhedruli*, contains more letters than the two historical ones, those extra letters are no longer needed for writing modern Georgian.

The Georgian kingdom of Iberia was converted to Christianity as early as the 330s AD. Most scholars believe that the first Old Georgian alphabet was modelled upon the Greek alphabet. The alphabet made it easier for the Georgians of that period to read religious scripture. This happened in the 4th or 5th century, not long after the conversion. The oldest uncontested example of Georgian writing is an *Asomtavruli* inscription from 430 AD in a church in Bethlehem.

Georgian historical tradition attributes the invention of the Georgian alphabet to one of the kings, Parnavaz I of Iberia in the 3rd century BC. Examples of the earliest alphabet, **Asomtavruli** (also known as *Mrgvlovani*), are still preserved in monumental inscriptions such as those of the Georgian church in Bethlehem (near Jerusalem 430 AD) and the church of Bolnisi Sioni near Tbilisi (4th-5th centuries). The **Nuskhuri** (ნუსხური "minuscule, lowercase") alphabet first appeared in the 9th century. It was mostly used in ecclesiastical works. **Nuskhuri** is related to the word **nuskha** (ნუსხა "inventory, schedule"). The currently used alphabet, called **Mkhedruli** (მხედრული, "cavalry" or "military"), first appeared in the 11th century. It was used for non-religious purposes up until the eighteenth century, when it completely replaced the *Khutsuri* style (that used the two previous alphabets). ***Mkhedruli*** is related to ***mkhedari*** (მხედარი, "horseman", "knight", or "warrior"); ***Khutsuri*** is related to ***khutsesi*** (ხუცესი, "elder" or "priest").

Georgian shared a common ancestral language with Svan and Mingrelian/Laz in the first millennium BC. Based on the degree of change, linguists (e.g. Klimov, T. Gamkrelidze, G. Machavariani) believe that the earliest split occurred in the second millennium BC or earlier, separating Svan from the other languages. Mingrelian and Laz separated from Georgian roughly a thousand years later.

The earliest allusion to spoken Georgian may be a passage of the Roman Grammarian Marcus Cornelius Fronto in the 2nd century AD: Fronto imagines the Iberians addressing the emperor Marcus Aurelius in their incomprehensible tongue.

The evolution of Georgian into a written language was a consequence of the conversion of the Georgian elite to Christianity in the mid-4th century. The new literary language was constructed on an already well-established cultural infrastructure of the functions, conventions, and status of Aramaic, the literary language of pagan Georgia and the new national religion. The first Georgian texts are inscriptions and palimpsests dating back to the 5th century.

Georgian has a rich literary tradition. The oldest surviving literary work in Georgian is the "Martyrdom of the Holy Queen Shushanik" (Tsamebay tsmidisa Shushanikisi dedoplisay) by Iakob Tsurtaveli, from the 5th century AD. The Georgian national epic, "The Knight in the Panther's Skin" (Vepkhistkaosani), by Shota Rustaveli, dates from the 12th century.

Reference: Hunt, D.G. (1999) *Georgian Folk Tales*, complied and translated into Russian by N.L. Dolidze, and from Russian into English by D.G. Hunt, Tbilisi, Merani Publishing House.

The Front Cover

The cover image is a file from the Wikimedia Commons. Information from its description page there is shown below. Commons is a freely licensed media file repository. A plague, on which is represented St. George rescuing the emperor's daughter. 15th century. In the past it belonged to the Botkin's collection, but was returned to Georgia in 1923. This is a faithful photographic reproduction of an original two-dimensional work of art. The work of art itself is in the public domain for the following reason: This image is in the public domain because its copyright has expired. This applies to Australia, the European Union and those countries with a copyright term of life of the author plus 70 years.

Notes on the authors

Michael Berman works as a teacher and a writer. Publications include *The Power of Metaphor* for Crown House, *The Nature of Shamanism and the Shamanic Story* for Cambridge Scholars Publishing, *Shamanic Journeys through the Caucasus* for O-Books, *Journeys Outside Time* for Pendraig Publishing, *Tales of Power* and *To and From the Land of the Dead* for Lear Books, and *Sacred Mountains* for Mandrake. For more information please visit www.Thestoryteller.org.uk

Manana Rusieshvili is a Full Professor and the Head of English Philology at Tbilisi State University. She is also the President of the English Teachers Association of Georgia (ETAG). Her research interests include pragmatics and sociolinguistics and she has published more than 40 articles, several textbooks and a monograph on semantics and pragmatics of Proverbs. Manana is also a teacher trainer approved by British Council and acts as an advisor to the Ministry of Education of Georgia and to the Tbilisi Municipal Government.

Ketevan Kalandadze is a teacher of Georgian as a Foreign Language, a translator, a founder of the Georgians Abroad Project (GAP), and a committee member of the British-Georgian Society. As if this was not enough, she also promotes both visual and performing artists from Georgia, Armenia, Azerbaijan, and the other independent states in the region, as well as artists from those countries now resident in the UK. Ketevan hopes that activities such as these will serve as a bridge between the Caucasus and the UK, helping to develop an appreciation of the rich, though relatively untapped, cultural heritage of the land where she was born.

Sometimes it seems to us mere mortals that there is little logic in this world we are born into, but what do we know? This is surely what this cautionary tale is all about. And although we may curse the seemingly adverse effects the elements may have on us at times, there is always a reason to be found for the apparent sense-lessness of it all:

The Hermit Philosopher

THERE was once a wise man who loved solitude, and dwelt far away from other men, meditating on the vanities of the world. He spent nearly all his time in the open air, and he could easily do this, for he lived in a lovely southern land where there is no winter and but little rain. As he wandered once among the verdure of his garden, the sage stopped before an aged walnut tree covered with ripening nuts, and said: "Why is there such a strange want of symmetry in nature? Here, for instance, is a walnut tree a hundred years old, hiding its top in the clouds, and yet how small is its fruit: itself it grows from year to year, but its fruit is always of the same size. Now, on the beds at the foot of the tree there grow great pumpkins and melons on very small creeping plants. It would be more fitting if the pumpkins grew on the walnut trees and the walnuts on the pumpkin beds. Why this want of symmetry in nature?" The sage thought deeply on the subject, and walked in the garden for a long time, till at last he felt sleepy. He lay down under the shady walnut tree, and was soon slumbering peacefully. In a short time, he felt a slight blow on the face, then a second, and then a third. As he opened his eyes, a ripe walnut fell on his nose. The sage leaped to his feet, and said: "Now I understand the secret of nature. If this tree had borne melons or pumpkins, my head would have been broken. Henceforth let no one presume to find fault with Providence!"

Taken from *Georgian Folk Tales*, by Marjory Wardrop [1894], at

This story comes from a short collection of folk tales from the nation of Georgia by Marjorie Wardrop, who also translated the Georgian author Rustaveli's *The Man in the Panther's Skin*. Although many of the motifs of these stories are also found in European folklore, there are characters and plot elements which localize them in the central Asian area.

* * *

What follows is an alternative version from the Caucasus of the same tale. Many teaching stories come from Sufi sources and are about a character called Mullah Nasrudin. Although several nations claim the Mullah as their own, like all mythological characters he belongs to everyone. The Mullah is a wise fool and his stories have many meanings on multiple levels of reality. The stories show that things are not always as they appear and often logic fails us.

Walnuts and Pumpkins

Nasrudin Hodja was lying in the shade of an ancient walnut tree. His body was at rest, but, befitting his calling as an imam, his mind did not relax. Looking up into the mighty tree he considered the greatness and wisdom of Allah.

"Allah is great and Allah is good," said the Hodja, "but was it indeed wise that such a great tree as this be created to bear only tiny walnuts as fruit? Behold the stout stem and strong limbs. They could easily carry the pumpkins that grow from spindly vines in yonder field, vines that cannot begin to bear the weight of their own fruit. Should not walnuts grow on weakly vines and pumpkins on sturdy trees?"

So thinking, the Hodja dozed off, only to be awakened by a walnut that fell from the tree, striking him on his forehead.

"Allah be praised!" he exclaimed, seeing what had happened. "If the world had been created according to my meagre wisdom, it would have been a pumpkin that fell from the tree and hit me on the head. It would have killed me for sure! Allah is great! Allah is good! Allah is wise!"

Never again did Nasrudin Hodja question the wisdom of Allah.

The Earth demands its Own

Once, in one of the villages of Georgia, there lived a widow. She had only one son who often asked why he did not have a father when all of his friends had dads. He used to question his mother: "Mum, Mum, if all of my friends have fathers, then why don't I? Where is my dad?"

"He is dead, my son!" Mum used to answer.

"Does that mean that he will never return? What is Death?" The boy would ask.

"No, my son, he will not come; We will go to him. Nobody can escape Death! One day we will all become the Earth when we die!"

"I did not ask God to bring me into this world! Why should I die if I do not want to?" asked the son. " I must find some place where there is no Death!"

Mum tried a lot to make him change his mind, but in vain!

The son travelled all over the world. Wherever he went, he asked if there was Death in that country. And the only reply he got everywhere was that yes, Death was known to everybody there.

The boy became very sad as he started to realize that there was not a single place on this Earth where there would be no Death! Time passed quickly and the boy became twenty years old.

Once, while walking in a vast field he came across a deer who had huge antlers branching up to the sky. The boy approached the deer and asked:

"May you always be blessed! Do you know any place unknown to Death?"

The deer answered:

"I am close to God and always follow his will. I will live until my antlers reach the Sky. As soon as this happens I will die! If you want to stay with me, you may do so and you will also live with me."

The boy said: "If I live, I should live forever! If I still have to die, why bother and travel so far?"

The boy continued his way past the fields, valleys and rocky hills. Finally, he arrived in a gorge in which the cliffs were so deep that one could not see its bottom. On the edge of the gorge sat a raven and time after time, it made a mess into the gorge. This raven was also following God's will.

The boy asked the raven if he knew a place in this Universe where Death was unknown to anyone.

The raven replied:

"God has ordered me to live until I fill up this gorge with my mess. If you wish, you can stay with me and you will also live till that time. Don't worry! You will be taken good care of and will not have to worry about anything."

The boy looked into the gorge but, in spite of it being huge and deep, he still thought that it was not big enough! Something hidden in his mind was urging him to move further!

So, the boy left the raven, walked past the land and reached the seashore. As he could not find a shallow place to cross the sea, he strolled up and down the shore for two days. When the third day came, he suddenly noticed something like a mirror sparkling from somewhere very far away! The boy walked in that direction and, when he came closer, he saw that what he had thought of as the sparkling thing, was actually a house made of crystal!

The boy was not able to find a door to the house. In the end, he noticed a little gap in the glass. He came closer and there it was – the door! He opened it and entered the room and lo! In the room there was the most beautiful girl he had ever seen – she was so beautiful that even the Sun would be jealous of her beauty.

The boy asked the girl: - "Beauty, I am running away from Death. Do you by chance know any place where nobody knows of him?"

The girl answered him: "There is nowhere without Death.

Stay here and be happy with me!"

But the boy replied that he did not mean to stay with her and the only thing he wished was to find the place without Death.

The girl said: "The Earth demands its own, and you would not like to live eternally!" Then she asked him how old she looked. The boy looked at her beautiful figure, cheeks like rose petals and forgot all about Death.

"You look about fifteen."

"No, I was born together with the World. My name is Beauty and will never grow old. Neither will I die. You could stay with me but alas! The Earth will demand you anyway."

The boy promised her that he would never leave her. They started living together and found great happiness.

Years flew away like minutes. A lot of things changed, the Earth changed, many died and many were born. This was known to everybody but the boy, who did not even notice how time flew. The girl was beautiful as always and the boy was equally handsome and young.

After a thousand years the boy suddenly realized that he was missing his country and longed to see his mother and relatives. He told the girl he had to go and see his mum and relatives once again.

Beauty did not want to let him go. She kept repeating that all of those people had been dead for centuries and he would not be able to see even their bones.

The boy replied: "What! This cannot be true! I have been here for only three or four days – how could they have all died?!"

The girl replied: "I have told you that the Earth would demand its own! All right, you can go but afterwards, blame yourself!"

Anyway, she gave him three apples and added that he should eat them when he got there.

The boy set off. While walking back he saw the familiar places. There was the gorge and the bottomless pit! The raven had died and was sitting all dried-up on the edge of the gorge full of his mess. The boy was devastated and recalled the girl's words. He wanted to go back but Fate did not let him do so. He went forward, passed the cliffs and found himself in the valley; he continued his way and what did he see? The deer had died as well, leaning with his antlers against the sky. Now, he was sure that a lot of time had passed. Still, he continued on his way to his motherland. When he got there, he was not able to find anyone alive that he knew when he was a child. He asked for his mum but nobody had even heard about her.

In the end, he came across one old man. The boy asked him about his mum and himself but the old man could not even believe him as he had heard that the story had happened thousands years before.

The people could not believe that he was alive and the rumour spread that the boy was sent from the other world. A lot of people followed him all wanting to talk to him. Finally, the boy reached the place where their house used to stand and what he saw were only the ruins of his childhood shelter grown over with yellow moss.

The boy recalled his mum, his childhood and grew so sad! In the end he remembered the apples and ate one of them. He did so and in just a minute his beard grew to his waist like moss, ate the second one and felt weakness in his knees. He could not even move. The boy hated himself for being so weak and dumb. Suddenly, he saw a little boy running around and called him over:

"Hey, boy! Can you help me to take an apple from my pocket?"

The boy did so. As soon as the old man had eaten it, he died. He was buried as a beggar by the village.

Translated from Georgian by Professor Manana Rusieshvili of Tbilisi State University, and edited by Michael Berman.

Insert picture here: A detail from St. George and the Dragon showing the dragon's head. Source: Cassell, Petter, Galpin & Co.: "Magazine of Art Illustrated" (1878) Status: out of copyright (called public domain in the USA), hence royalty-free stock image for all purposes.

What the Earth means to Georgians

Just after God created the earth, he called all the peoples and nations to assemble on a certain day, so each could be presented with a homeland. All the nations dutifully showed up, except the Georgians. God parcelled out a piece of the earth to each nation, and then, weary from the task, he started home. On the way he came across the Georgians, sitting on the grass under a tree, drinking wine and singing.

"Why didn't you come to the Giving of the Homelands?" God asked. "Now you have none for yourselves."

The Georgians were crestfallen. "We're sorry, God," they said. "We were on our way, but we were so impressed by the beauty of this world that we stopped to drink a toast to the grass and the trees. Then we drank toasts to the sun and to the blue waters and to the high mountains. In fact we spent the whole day here, singing and drinking to the loveliness of your creation."

God was touched. "Well," he said, "there is still one little piece of earth left, the most beautiful of all. I was saving it for myself. But since you know so well how to appreciate it, you shall have it, and it shall be called Georgia."

* * *

They say that God works in mysterious ways, and he/she certainly seems to do so in the tale that follows, or is it we ourselves who do? I will leave it to you, the reader, to decide:

The Field of Salt

The village of Lahitsch lies in the mountains far from any town, and so the villagers are often in need of various things, and particularly of salt. In order to remedy this misfortune, two of the villagers – two brothers – made up their minds to sow salt, then they would never again need to go to town for salt, and they could perhaps make money by selling it as well. No sooner said than done. A large field was sown with salt. When spring came, it lay there black and naked while all the fields around it were green and fertile.

"Why in the world does our salt not come up?" said one of the brothers to the other: "perhaps someone has stolen it from us. We will look and see." And so they wandered away down to their field of salt, and found there a great swarm of flies of the kind generally to be met with on saltish ground.

"There we are! They have eaten up our salt! Shoot them dead, shoot them dead!" And a tremendous firing began.

When they were tired of shooting, they sat down to rest and have a bite of food. The flies came round them, and one, who was very bold, sat on the brow of one of the brothers. "Sit quite quiet, without moving," the other brother told him. He took his gun, aimed carefully and shot the fly quite dead.

Taken from *Caucasian Folk-tales*: Selected and Translated from the originals by Adolf Dirr. Translated into English by Lucy Menzies. 1925 London & Toronto J.M. Dent & Sons Ltd.

In Communist times in Georgia everyone automatically had a job and nobody needed to go in search of one. However, since the fall of Communism and the establishment of the independent Republic of Georgia, the enormous changes that are being experienced have taken the older generation by surprise and they are still finding it hard to come to terms with them. To take full advantage of the newly established freedom, those same people now need to be pro-active, perhaps for the very first time, for it is a skill they never needed to develop before. While the new generation are finding it easier to adapt, the older are really struggling, and this story carries a message for them – that your fate is very much in your own hands now, and if you're willing to work the earth, then it will bear fruit for you. However, if you are not prepared to take control of your life, then the victim of circumstance that you believe you are today is what you will always be:

The story is an adaptation of the version of *Fortune* translated from the Russian by D. G. Hunt that can found in Dolidze, N.I. (1999) *Georgian Folk Tales*, Tbilisi: Merani Publishing House. Professor Hunt has translated numerous folktales from the Caucasus, and we are greatly indebted to him for donating so much of his work to the British Library, thereby making it more widely available.

Fortune

It happened or it did not happen – in a certain land there lived a cattle-breeder. He was honest, hardworking, and he never offended anybody. All his animals grazed contentedly without being watched, and neither beast nor man hurt them, since he had no enemies.

In that same land lived a certain lazybones and idler. He did not do anything. While others were working, he was sleeping, so that he lived in poverty and only blamed it on his fate.

So one day that cattle-breeder met him. He greeted the poor man and asked, "How's life with you, friend?"

"What sort of life do I have?" he began to moan and groan, "I'm dying of hunger".

"Let's go to my place", said the cattle-breeder. "Work for me for a year and I'll give you a pair of good oxen. Then you can plough and sow your own field, and you'll be satisfied".

The idler thought, "Why work for him to overstrain myself for a pair of oxen? I might as well help myself and just take whatever I want. They say that the cattle even graze without being watched; so who's going to stop me?"

He climbed into the mountains, and he saw the cattle scattered across the land, but of herdsmen, there was none. He looked at this wealth, and his heart became just sick with envy. He had just got close when suddenly something began to ring, and all the animals started to run to the other side of the meadow where they gathered together in one place.

The idler also approached. He saw, standing in the middle of the cattle, a tiny little man. And the cows and sheep were gathered all around him. Some licked his face, some his hand, and he caressed them and stroked their hair.

The idler was surprised, and he asked, "Who are you? What sort of creature are you? Where have you been and where did you suddenly appear from?"

"I'm the fortune of the master of this herd", says the little man. "However, I also look after all his cattle, and I don't let anybody disturb them".

"And where then is my fortune?" asked the poor man.

"Your fortune can be found on such and such a mountain under such and such a bush", says this little man.

"And will I find my fortune if I go there?"

"Why ever shouldn't you find him, certainly you'll find him!" said the little man.

Somehow the idler got to the mountain indicated. He searched and searched for his fortune, but no way could he find it. He got tired, and he lay down in distress under a tree and dozed off. He slept through really soundly and when he woke up the sun was already setting. Suddenly he heard somebody sighing. He got up and looked: "Who is it sighing like that?" He saw, lying under bush, a little man: just skin and bone. He was lying there, groaning, and sighing.

"Who are you? What sort of creature are you and why are you lying about here?" asked the idler.

"But I'm your fortune", said the little man.

"Ach, you, lazybones!" the idler said angrily. "Whatever sort of fortune are you to me if all you do is lie here and groan? I'm dying of hunger, and you make a habit of lying down; and as for thinking about me, you don't think at all."

"You're a good man", said this fortune. "You lie down and sleep, and I lie down and sleep. You sit and do nothing, and I do even more so. Get up and make some effort! Do some work, and I'll reward you. And your life will change for the better."

So the poor man finally got the message and began to work. And for the first time in his life he stood on his own two feet. He got married, started a family of his own and began to live free of cares.

Our stay on Earth is all over so quickly that we need to ensure we make the most of it. That is what the final tale in this section is surely intended to make us reflect on:

Death visits Earth

There was a childless man living in poverty in a certain village who did not have anybody to look after in this world. However, he still worked hard in the fields from morning till night and when it got dark, he would lean his heavy hoe against the hedge of his garden, go into his small hut, kindle the fire in the fireplace, take a cold maize scone from his only cupboard and nibble on that and a little fish. Later, he would go to bed but instead of falling asleep, one and the same nightmare would always torture him. In his dream he saw his mother dragging him to the Other World, where only the dead lived. That is why he was terrified of death.

Once, Death mounted his white horse and descended to Earth. He was looking after the people who he would take to the Other World. As Death was galloping along the road, he came across our poor childless man who, upon seeing him, became so frightened that he even tried to hide behind the shrubs and bushes at the side of the road. Anyway, Death had noticed him and galloping closer he greeted him. The man, still white with fear, returned the greeting.

"Don't be afraid because I haven't come for you on this occasion. I have to take a couple of other people from this village with me though, and while I'm looking for them, I was wondering if you could look after my horse," asked Death.

The man took the saddle of the horse in his hand and, as Death went to collect the people he was after, he thought to himself: Wouldn't it be a good idea to steal this horse and ride away with it? For if Death didn't have the horse, how would he take people on his list to the Other World? And if I did so, I would save a lot of people from dying that way!

The man mounted the horse but he was not able to ride it as Death had taken his whip with him and the horse did not obey whoever rode it without being whipped first. Soon Death was back, bringing along several youngsters he was planning to take back with him. When he saw the man on his horse, he started to laugh in surprise and asked him if he intended to steal his horse. The man did not have any excuse to offer as this was precisely what he was going to do. Death laughed again, gave the whip to the man and said:

"Whip the horse and it will fly you high up into the sky. And, when you come back again, tell me what you have seen".

The man followed Death's instructions and the horse took him up into the sky, just as he had told him it would. They flew for a long time to and fro and when they returned, Death asked the man what he had seen up there

"Nothing" answered the man. "But what shocked me was when I looked down and saw Earth from up there because it looked no larger than an egg."

Death laughed again and then said this:

"Now, if you can see that Earth is as small as an egg, do you really think I wouldn't be able to find you even without my horse? This time I'll let you off, but next time you might not be so lucky so you should never think about doing any more dishonest deeds!"

Death then mounted his horse, together with the boys and girls he intended to take with him, and disappeared.

As for the poor man, he was left at the side of the road to reflect on the significance of everything that had happened to him that day.

An Ossetian Folktale: Alaguai

First of all, before presenting the story, some background information on the region. North Ossetia-Alania is one of the
sovereign republics of the Russian Federation and is situated on
the northern slopes of the central Caucasus between two of the
highest mountain peaks in Europe, Elbrous (5613m) and
Kazbeck (5047m). It is one of the smallest, most densely
populated and multi-cultural republics, with an area of 8,000
square kilometres (3,088.8 sq ml).

As for the people, they are "the distant descendants and last
representatives of the northern Iranians whom the ancients
called Scythians and Sarmatians and who, at the dawn of the
Middle Ages, under the name of the Alani and Roxolani, made
Europe quake with fear" (Bonnefoy, 1993, p.262).

The ancestors of the Ossetians were the Alans, and the Daryal
Gorge takes its name from them ("Dar-i-Alan", Gate of the
Alans). They wandered as nomads over the steppes watered by
the Terek, Kuban and Don Rivers until the Huns, under Attila,
swept into Europe and split them into two parts. One group of
the Alans moved into Western Europe; along with another
wandering people, the Vandals, they passed through Spain into
North Africa, where they disappear from history (Pearce, 1954,
p.12).

The other group were forced southwards and eventually
settled along the Terek, immediately north of the main Caucasus
Range. There they entered into trading and cultural relations
with other people of the Black Sea region, and in the tenth
century were converted to Christianity.

In the last years of the Soviet Union, as nationalist movements
swept throughout the Caucasus, many intellectuals in the North
Ossetian ASSR called for the revival of the name of Alania, a
medieval kingdom of the Alans, ancestors of the modern-day

Ossetians. The term "Alania" quickly became popular in Ossetian daily life, so much so that in November 1994, "Alania" was added to the official name, which became the Republic of North Ossetia-Alania.

The population of North Ossetia today is predominantly Christian with a large Muslim minority, speaking Ossetic and Russian. Despite the predominant religion being Russian Orthodox Christianity, followed by Islam, many of the native rituals predate both faiths.

The most popular element of the animist-pagan tradition is the cult of Wasterzhi and his sacred grove about 30 kilometres from the capital Vladikavkaz. Part protector of warriors and travellers, part phallic symbol, Wasterzhi is a mysterious character whose origins have been linked to Indo-Iranian sun worship, star worship, war gods and the ancient Nart heroes of the Caucasus. A painting often seen reproduced on posters depicts him as a medieval knight with a long beard on a white stallion with sizeable testicles.

Hoping to fully convert the Ossetians, the Russian Orthodox Church encouraged Christian saints as replacements for Wasterzhi and the rest of the extensive pagan pantheon, headed by Khusaw, the Almighty. But instead of abandoning their gods, the Ossetians fused them with the saints, creating hybrid deities subservient to Khusaw and Christianity's God. Wasterzhi's alter ego was Saint George, and Wasilla, the god of harvests and thunder, became interchangeable with Saint Illya.

No priests are required in the popular Ossetian faith. Against a background of heavy feasting and many religious vodka toasts, Ossetian families and villages will sacrifice sheep and bulls to these lesser divinities and implore their help (Smith, 2006, p.81). The first toast is always to the head god, who is known as "Khutsauty Khutsau ('god of gods'), or simply Khutsau, like Anc°a among the Abkhasians or Morige among the Georgians, does not intervene directly in human affairs but delegates his powers to minor deities" (Bonnefoy, 1993, p.262).

The legend behind the sacred grove outside Vladikavkaz is that a certain Hetag was fleeing his enemies in the 14th to 16th centuries when Wasterzhi called out from the mountain forest and told him to shelter there. Exhausted, Hetag collapsed on the plains, saying he could not go on, whereupon a clump of trees (today's wood) miraculously came down and hid him ... Ever since, the grove has been a living cathedral for Wasterzhi, a memorial to Hetag, and an open-air chapel for Saint George.

[T]he wood, best known as Hetag's Grove, is deeply venerated. It is largely made up of ashes and beeches, covering just under 13 hectares in a roughly triangular shape. A temple with a large wooden totem pole has been built nearby, alongside a ... banqueting hall for the yearly festivals, where each village is assigned its own tree and clearing.

Believers who pass the grove along the main road, about a kilometre away, rise out of their seats and mumble a few prayers to Wasterzhi, while once in the wood it is forbidden to break off even a single branch. Holy trees are decorated with ribbons and portraits of Saint George and the dragon. And because of his fertility powers, women are forbidden from saying either Hetag or the W word (Smith, pp.81-82).

When atheism was in force in Soviet times, there was a real barrier to local traditions, but even then, the head of the household would still gather his family and pray to Wasterzhi and drink a toast, and the tradition has both survived and flourished against all the odds.

Despite the inevitable economic burden of a sizeable refugee population, North Ossetia is the most well-to-do republic in the northern Caucasus. It is the most urbanized and the most industrialized, with factories producing metals (lead, zinc, tungsten, etc.), electronics, chemicals, and processed foods. The Republic also has abundant mineral resources and its numerous mountain rivers serve as an important source of electric power. More than half of the territory of the Republic is occupied by high mountains, rich in deciduous and coniferous woods, as well as alpine pastures.

The territory of North Ossetia has been inhabited for thousands of years by the Vainakh tribes, being both a very fertile agricultural region and a key trade route through the Caucasus Mountains. The ancestors of the present inhabitants were a people called the Alans, a warlike nomadic people who spoke an Iranian language. Part of the Alan people eventually settled in the Caucasus around the 7th century AD. By about the 9th century, the kingdom of Alania had arisen and had been converted to Christianity by Byzantine missionaries. Alania became a powerful state in the Caucasus, profiting greatly from the legendary Silk Road to China, which passed through its territory.

Polytheism is characteristic of the world of beliefs of nomads, and the Samartian Alans were no exception to this. Batraz was the Alan god of war, and there was also a mother goddess who was the equivalent of the Greek Potnia Theron. As for the cult of the Sun and the Moon, beside altars dated from the end of the 6th and the beginning of the 5th centuries BC, smoking vessels have been found. It is highly likely that the people who took part in the rituals would have been overcome by the smoke produced from these vessels, and that this could have resulted in them entering altered states of consciousness, which is of course what shamans frequently did (see Vaday, 2002, pp.215-221).

From the Middle Ages onwards, Alania was beset by external enemies and, due to its strategic geographical position, suffered repeated invasions. The invasions of the Mongols and Tatars in the 13th century decimated the population, who were now known as Ossetians. Islam was introduced in the 17th century through the Kabardians, a Muslim Caucasian people. Incursions by the Khanate of Crimea and the Ottoman Empire eventually pushed Alania/Ossetia into an alliance with Russia in the 18th century.

North Ossetia was among the first areas of the northern Caucasus to come under Russian domination, starting in 1774, and the capital, Vladikavkaz, was the first Russian military outpost in the region. By 1806, Ossetia was completely under Russian control. The arrival of the Russians led to the rapid development of the region, with industries founded and road and rail connections built to overcome Ossetia's isolation. The Georgian Military Road, which is still a crucial transport link across the mountains, was built in 1799 and a railway line was built from Vladikavkaz to Rostov-on-Don in Russia proper. The Ossetians' traditional culture inevitably underwent some russification, but their new connections with Russia and the West helped to boost local culture; the first books in the Ossetian language were printed in the late 18th century. Ossetia became part of the Terskaya Region of Russia in the mid-19th century.

During and after the war Stalin undertook massive deportations of whole ethnicities explaining this by anti-Sovietism, separatism and collaboration with Nazi Germany. In particular, this affected Balkars, Chechens, and Ingush. As of 1944, the part of the Prigorodny District on the right bank of the Terek River had been part of Chechen-Ingush SSR, but it was granted to North Ossetia following Stalin's deportation of the Chechens and Ingush to Central Asia. Although they were eventually allowed to return from exile, they were generally not allowed to settle in the original territories.

North Ossetian SSR finally became the first autonomous republic of the RSFSR to declare national sovereignty, on June 20, 1990 (although it still remains firmly part of Russia). In 1991 it was renamed the Republic of North Ossetia-Alania.

The dissolution of the Soviet Union posed particular problems for the Ossetian people who, at the time, were divided between North Ossetia, which was part of the Russian SFSR, and South Ossetia, part of the Georgian SSR. However, it is a widespread view among Ossetians themselves that though, on the one hand,

> the aspirations of South Ossetians to join their Northern tribesmen can be understood from the human viewpoint, from the geopolitical viewpoint it can be regarded as a mistake. The main Caucasus Ridge is a natural border between Georgia and Ossetia and any efforts to remove this border is therefore likely to result in a conflict developing between Georgians and Ossets. To restore traditional friendly relations, first of all, the talk on the separation of Ossetia from Georgia would have to stop. No authorities representing Georgia would agree to this in any case. And they would be right to reject such a separation because this would result in a violation of Georgia's territorial integrity... Anyone who wants peace between the South Ossetians and Georgians, should reject forever the idea of South Ossetia's joining North Ossetia. Anyone who hopes for peace between Georgia and Russia, should also put this idea aside. This is the reality of the situation **Vasili Abayev** - famous Ossetian professor and renowned scholar [the unedited quote, without corrections to the translation, can be found at http://darbr.webs.com/theos-setsingeorgia.htm].

In spite of these foreboding words, in December 1990 the conflict between Georgia and South Ossetia, which led to refugees fleeing both to other parts of Georgia and to North Ossetia, was kindled anyway. The latter led to an Ossetian-Ingush conflict. North Ossetia also had to deal with refugees and the occasional spillover of fighting from the war in neighbouring Chechnya. The bloodiest incident by far was the September 2004 Beslan hostage crisis, in which in the firefight between the Chechen terrorists and Russian forces that ended this blood-shedding crisis, 335 civilians, the majority of them children, died.

People who believed in Georgian and Ossetian friendship,

good relations and goodwill, still hoped that these two nations would be able to find some kind of common ground for negotiations. However, in the summer of 2008, the Georgian-Russian war put an end to such hopes and expectations. There are two main interpretations of what took place and why: one is that on 7 August, after a series of low-level clashes in the region, Georgia tried to retake South Ossetia by force. Russia launched a counter-attack and the Georgian troops were ousted from both South Ossetia and Abkhazia. The other interpretation, and the one most Georgians believe to be the case, is that the whole situation was not in fact so simple, that the war between Russia and Georgia did not start on that day, and that the "volcano" that erupted had been smouldering beneath the surface for many years prior to the actual events taking place.

If we recall the period preceding the war, it will become evident that the situation was particularly escalated after the NATO Bucharest meeting where Georgia was not given MAP, though it was announced that NATO would help Georgia to become a member one day. It is believed that this event encouraged Russia to throw its additional forces into Abkhasia under the excuse of rebuilding the railway system at the same time escalating the situation in Ossetia where Georgian villages were constantly bombarded and ruined. On the 7th of August around 15, 000 Russian soldiers and tanks crossed into Georgian territory via the Rock tunnel from North Ossetia and from Abkhasia via Psou. Georgian towns situated beyond the conflict zone were bombed, namely Gori, Poti, and Zugdidi, and the Russians could have gone on to attack Tbilisi too, but were apparently dissuaded from doing so after Sarkozy's intervention. However, whatever the reason for the war, Russia still holds the Georgian territory which they occupied, in spite of being urged by many European and American leaders to withdraw their forces. Moreover, Russia is still the only country to recognize the independence of the two breakaway regions of Georgia. The rest of the world, however, has not followed suit, and what the future will bring remains uncertain at this point. One thing is certain, people in Georgia (and not only in Georgia) firmly believe that if Russia had not stirred up the conflicts and discontent in the region in the first place, the South Ossetians and the Georgians could well be living peacefully side by side now.

Alaguai

There lived a very poor husband and wife, and they had nothing. In the end, they got so tired of being hungry that they decided to go and work as servants for a rich nobleman. The husband worked as a shepherd, the wife washed laundry, and they lived in a small dilapidated shack. Soon they had a son and called him Alaguai. But when Alaguai was seven years old his father passed away. The boy wanted to bury his father with the respect that was due to him and this is what he said to his mother:

"You have to arrange a kelekhi (a meal served to all the mourners after a funeral) after we bury my father!"

The mother was surprised to hear this request from her seven-year-old son. After the funeral, Alaguai started to work as a shepherd in place of his father. Exactly seven years later his mother passed away too. Alguai buried her mother, showing her the same respect as he did to his father. He worked one more year for the rich nobleman and then this is what he said:

"My parents and I have been serving you for fifteen years now, and the time has come to pay me everything we have earned during that time."

The nobleman replied:

"The problem is you have no idea how much both of your parents' funerals cost me. I've calculated what they earned and I'm telling you, that on the contrary, it's your parents who owe me. Out of the kindness of my heart, I'll let you off paying that money back though, and give you one year's salary instead."

Alaguai realized that the nobleman was cheating him, he got angry, and left without a penny. While walking he saw an old woman crying bitterly.

"Why are you crying mother?" He asked.

"Because all my life I served that ungrateful nobleman, but now he's sacked me. He says it's because I've grown too old. And now I'm left with nobody in this world and I don't know where to go or what to do."

"I've got nobody either," he replied. "And I'm in exactly the same situation as you. So let's find somewhere to live together."

So they walked and walked until they came to a dark forest, where they decided to stay for the night. When the sun rose the next morning, they saw a beautiful woman bathing in a lake full of milk.

"That girl is the daughter of the sun," the old woman said to Alaguai. "And if you can catch and marry her, we'll have no problem at all getting revenge on the unjust nobleman who treated us both so badly."

"I'll go to find the sun's daughter then," was what Alaguai said. "And I want you to wait here for me for a year. But if I don't return then, it means I'll be dead."

Alaguai left. On his way he saw a pack of wild dogs chasing a fox. The fox spoke to Alaguai, in a human voice, and this is what he said:

"Save me and I'll help you to find your fortune!"

The boy drove the dogs away and saved the fox. The fox plucked out a tuft of his fur and gave it to Alaguai.

"Here's a tuft of my fur," he said. "When you need some help singe it in a fire. And when the scent of it reaches me, I'll appear in front of you the very same moment."

The boy carried on walking. He saw that some hunters had caught an eagle and were getting ready to kill it. The eagle spoke to Alaguai, in a human voice, and this is what he said:

"Save me and I'll help you to find your fortune!"

The boy saved the eagle. The eagle plucked out one of its feathers with its beak, gave it to Alaguai and said:

"Here's one of my feathers. When you need some help singe it in a fire. And when the scent of it reaches me, I'll appear in front of you the very same moment."

The boy carried on walking. He walked and walked and came to the lake once more. He saw some fishermen trying to catch a big fish there. The fish spoke to Alaguai, in a human voice, and this is what he said:

"Save me and I'll help you to find your fortune!"

The boy saved the fish. The fish gave the boy a bone and said:

"Here's one of my bones. When you need some help singe it in a fire. And when the scent of it reaches me, I'll appear in front of you the very same moment."

Alaguai kept the bone and carried on walking. He saw a high gate which had poles all around it. Each pole had a skull fixed on it, except for one. The boy was surprised but opened the gate in any case and went in. He saw an old man there:

"Tell me father. Why does each pole have a human skull on it?" He asked.

"The daughter of the sun lives here," the old man replied. "Lots of young men come here from all over the world in the hope of marrying her. But her nanny kills them all. These are the skulls of all those young men who tried to marry her before. The nanny is looking for a bridegroom who can hide so they cannot find him, and will give each applicant three chances only to succeed."

Alaguai had no fear though, and decided to ask the nanny to give him a chance.

"OK you can take her, was the nanny's response, "but on one condition. You have to hide without us finding you and you have three chances only. But if you fail, you'll die, and it will be your skull that decorates that final pole."

The boy agreed. Alaguai went to the lake, made a fire by the side of it and put the fish bone on it. Suddenly the water in the lake became agitated, and the very same fish the boy had saved earlier on his journey appeared.

"What's wrong Alaguai? Do you need help by any chance?"

"Yes, I want to marry the daughter of the sun. But I have to hide so that nobody can find me. If her nanny finds me, I'll be beheaded. If not, I can marry her."

"Come close to me then," said the fish.

The fish opened its mouth, swallowed Alaguai, and then swam off. From the lake, it swam into an ocean and hid in the sand under the ocean. The girl and the nanny looked for him with the sun's mirror and found him in the stomach of the fish.

The fish swam back, opened his mouth, and let the boy out. Alaguai went to the nanny and asked:

"Did you find me then?"

"Yes, we did. You were hiding in the stomach of a fish under the sand in the ocean," she said.

He was given a second chance. Alaguai made another fire, and burned the feather of the eagle this time. Suddenly the very same eagle the boy had saved earlier on his journey appeared.

"What's wrong Alaguai? Do you need help by any chance?"

"Yes, I want to marry the daughter of the sun. But I have to hide so that nobody can find me. If the nanny of the daughter finds me, I'll be beheaded. If not, I can marry her."

"Come sit on my back and I'll hide you," said the eagle.

So Alaguai sat on the eagle's back. It flew up into the sky, attached him to the roof of the sky, and covered him with its wings.

The daughter of the sun and nanny looked into the sun's mirror and saw him in the sky though.

The boy returned again the next day.

"We know you were hiding under the wings of the eagle in the sky," said the nanny.

He was given his third and final chance to hide. Alaguai went, made a fire, and burned the tuft of fur the fox had given him. And the very same fox came to him once again.

"What's wrong Alaguai? Do you need help by any chance?"

"Yes, I do, I want to marry the daughter of the sun. But I have to hide so that nobody can find me. If the nanny of the daughter finds me I'll be beheaded. If not I can marry her. I've had two chances already but they found me each time. Now I'm on my last chance, and it all depends on you."

"Go and ask them to give you three days," said the fox.

So Alaguai asked for three days and nanny agreed.

The fox started to dig up the earth under the cliffs, hid the dug-out soil near the river, then brought Alaguai to the tunnel he had made, and said:

"Go and walk as far as you can!"

Alaguai entered the tunnel. It led to the bottom of the cliff where the sun's daughter lived. The fox lay down to cover the entry to the tunnel so that nobody could see it. The daughter of the sun and the nanny looked up to the sky, looked down to the waters but failed to notice him hiding just under their own feet. Then they admitted they had lost the bet.

So Alaguai married the daughter of the sun and took her home. On the way they met the fish again:

"You'll meet a cloud on your way," the fish said. "Don't touch it or you'll die!"

Alaguai carried on walking and met the eagle again:

"You'll meet a cloud on the way, but don't touch it," the eagle said. "Here's a whistle for you. But don't touch the cloud with your hands or you'll die!"

Alaguai carried on walking and this time met the fox again:

"You'll see a cloud in front of you shortly," the fox said. "Take this dagger. But don't touch the cloud with your hands or you'll die!"

Just as they had been warned, they saw the cloud on their way. The daughter of the sun said to him:

"It's my nanny. Do as you were told or you'll lose me forever."

Alaguai used his dagger, blew the whistle, and the cloud disappeared. But water drops came down. These are the very same drops that come down when it rains, even now!

Alaguai and the sun's daughter left and went to the lake where Alaguai had left the old woman. They spent a wonderful time there and afterwards they all went to the rich nobleman's place together. Alaguai killed him and lived in the nobleman's home in his place. All the lands he gave to the poor and that way Alaguai and the sun's daughter gave them their freedom. So let nothing hurt you until they get here!

Taken from *Ossetian Tales and Legends*, published in Tskhinvali by Iristoni Publishing House in 1972. Translated by Ketevan Kalandadze.

References

Berman, M. (2009) *Shamanic Journeys through the Caucasus*, Hampshire: O-Books.

Bonnefoy, Y. (comp.) (1993). *American, African and Old European Mythologies*. Chicago and London, The University of Chicago Press.

King, C. (2008). *The Ghost of Freedom*. New York: Oxford University Press Inc.

Matveena, A. (1999). *The North Caucasus: Russia's Fragile Borderland*. London: The Royal Institute of International Affairs.

Pearce, B. (1954). "The Ossetians In History." In Rothstein, A. (Ed.) (1954), *A People Reborn: The Story of North Ossetia*, 12-17. London: Lawrence & Wishart.

Smith, S. (2006). *Allah's Mountains: The Battle for Chechnya*. London: Tauris Parke Paperbacks.

Vaday, A. (2002). "The World of Beliefs of the Sarmatians." A Nograd Megyei Muzeumok Evkonyve XXVI.

The Return of Fire

In times long, long ago, when the lands of Abkhazia were completely covered with thick forests, and the mountains showed green under the rays of the hot sun, there were living here good-looking and strong people. They lived harmoniously and with enjoyment. Nature endowed them generously with fruits and the meats of wild animals. The clean rivers bore their cool waters to these people. In a word, they were living carefree lies, for it did not take a lot of work to obtain food or to find shelter. Abkhazia then was a land of abundance. And one thing which these people valued, which they guarded more than their own eyes, was the fire, which had already burned hundreds of years on the summit of a hill. The people did not let it go out, for among them existed the superstition: if they do not have fire, they will not have a happy life.

But one day it happened that a downpour extinguished the eternal flame. A careless fellow-tribesman had not looked after it. The people came to the hill and saw with horror that instead of the hot flame in the sacred hearth, a pitiful puff of smoke was coming from it. And then a great lament began among the people. The hearth had gone out for ever. And the people? As before, they gave way to weeping and moaning, for they piously believed in the prediction of their ancestors. Then the oldest and most experienced man among them got up and asked the people whether anybody knew the secret of obtaining fire. Their answer to him was silence.

"Then we are going to perish", said the old man. "But isn't there a daredevil among us who would get a small piece of the burning-hot sun from the sky?"

The people looked at one another in bewilderment. "No, such a person can't be found amongst us, he can't be found", they were whispering.

But suddenly the crowd stirred and made way, and a very handsome youth came out from the middle.

"It is Amra, he is called Amra", they began saying all round. They knew Amra well. The young man was the embodiment of beauty and courage.

"I will get a little piece of the sun!", said he firmly. "One day we have lost the fire, but we can find it once more. But a little piece of the sun – isn't this too much for a small people?"

"No, no!" the people began shouting. "Use our hands, Amra, to help you, only get what you promised for us as quickly as you can".

"All right", said the young man.

For three days and three nights the people were making a gigantic bow under Amra's guidance. This bow was hundreds and hundreds of loktey in height (one lokot, plural loktey, is equal to a cubit, or about 50cm). And they twisted the string for it from the tendons of a thousand oxen. At last, on the expiry of the third night, the people raised the gigantic bow with an arrow, on the summit of the highest mountain, Ertsakhu. And by that time the sun was already standing at the zenith. Thousands of people stretched the string. Amra carefully aimed. And a miracle happened: the arrow hit directly in the centre of the sun. The sun began trembling with the pain, dropping a little tear. Very soon the little tear reached the ground, and a thousand-year-old forest burst into hot flame. The valleys of our land were covered with smoke for three months. There were many fires, but the forests vanished, the prey animals were burned alive, and the rivers became shallow.

"You have got our fire back, but you have deprived us of food", the people reproached Amra.

"Now we cannot live comfortably. Leave us, young man who has brought us bad luck".

"All right", said Amra, "I will leave. And may the sorrow that has settled in your hearts vanish together with me".

Amra spoke thus and instantly changed into a sunray which began playing on a baby's face. Since that time the forests grow plentifully in our land only in the foothills. But on the other hand, the land at the foot of the mountains is rich and fertile. And here various fruits spring up, and the people will dwell happily under the sun which is called in Abkhazian "Amra."

* * *

Taken from Pachulia, V.P. (1986) The fall of Anakopia: Legends and Traditions of the Caucasus Black-Sea Coastal Region, Moscow: "NAUKA" Publishing House (Translated from the Russian by D.G.Hunt.

Amra was the ancient Abkhazian pagan deity of the sun. So strong was the worship of this deity that even at the time of the construction of the Orthodox Pskal church in the early Middle Ages on the conical summit of the Mountain Pskal, a craftsman has drawn his image in the altar barrier.

* * *

In recent years in Abkhazia a growth of neo-paganism has been observed. Pagan traditions in the region had never disappeared completely, so there was no need to invent too much by reference to books, as almost all the resources were still intact.

During the period of upheaval that accompanied the break-up of the Soviet Union, and especially during the Georgian-Abkhazian War, many Abkhazians sought solace in religion. However, for most the acceptance of Christianity was merely superficial and today the number of parishioners attending services is quite insignificant, even on important feast days.

On the other hand, a large number of people have a shrine, or anykha (smithy), in their family's village, the worship of which can be traced back to the ancient cults of fire and metal. Such 'domestic' shrines belong to everyday life, but people appeal to more revered, 'powerful' anykha in more critical situations. The latter include the shrines Dydrypsh-nykha, Yebyr-nykha, Lapyr-nykha, Lashkendar, Ldzaa-nykha, Lykh-nykha and Ylyr-nykha. And the syncretic consciousness that prevails among Abkhazians today is clearly illustrated by the fact that for many, whether they consider themselves to be Muslim or Christian, the main god is still Dydrypsh who inhabits Dydrypsh-nykha mountain.

The preservation of the major role played by traditional cults is primarily explained by the fact that they have great significance in the lives of Abkhazian families and clans. In family and clan gatherings the elder takes on the role of priest and, after sacrificing an animal, appeals to the great god Anshchshchyua (this is the exact spelling, unlike Antsea or Antsva as is written today) with a request to remove misfortunes, illnesses and other inflictions from all his relatives, to prolong, increase and bless the clan, and other similar wishes. Afterwards each member of the clan repeats the prayer, eats a bite from the cooked liver and heart of the sacrificial animal and drinks a glass of holy wine which has been specially prepared for the ceremony. There is then a meal comprising the meat of the sacrificial animal and other dishes which have been prepared and arranged in a strictly defined manner. Abkhazians begin to take part in such ceremonies and feasts from a very early age, and they are an extremely effective means of consolidating the cohesion of family and clan.

Interest in Paganism among the Abkhazian people can in fact be seen to have developed in two different environments:

Firstly, in the countryside with its unbroken continuity of traditional folk beliefs, and secondly, in the urbanized areas where local, highly secularized intellectuals began to construct a new synthetic religion in order to overcome a crisis of identity. In the latter case, this was a manifestation of local ethnic nationalism (Shnirelman, 2002).

So neo-paganism in Abkhazia today flourishes, especially

since the Georgian–Abkhazian war of 1992–1993. Not only does it flourish, but it is also protected by the Abkhazian authorities.

In particular, the latter took part in the bull sacrifice in October 1993 in order to thank the Lord for the victory over the Georgians. The Abkhazians believe that their ethnic god Dydrypsh awarded them the victory. Since then, the Abkhazian leaders have regularly taken part in traditional rituals (Shnirelman, 2002).

Neo-pagan practices are thus in part being promoted to support a nationalistic political agenda and to justify the continued quest for independence from Georgia.

Reference

Shnirelman, V.A. (2002) 'Christians! Go home: A Revival of Neo-Paganism between the Baltic Sea and Transcaucasia (An Overview).' In Journal of Contemporary Religion, Vol. 17, No. 2, 2002

Tlepsh and Lady Tree from the Forest of Circassia

In the southernmost part of European Russia, near the border of the Soviet Union with Turkey and Iran rise the highest mountains in Europe, the mighty massif of the Caucasus. In the complex topography of this region live many tribes and ethnic groups, most of whom speak languages unrelated to any others on earth. One of these groups with a distinctive language is that of the Circassians (Colarusso, J. 1989 'Myths from the Forest of Circassia.' In The World & I, December, 1989. The Washington, D.C.: The Washington Times Publishing Corporation. Pp. 644-651).

The veneration of trees and forests was once commonplace in the region and is reflected in the story that follows, adapted from a tale in the collection of Circassian Nart sagas by the Soviet scholar Asker Hadaghat'la.

* * *

As god of fire and the forge Tlepsh had been very kind to the Narts, inventing many useful tools and implements for them. However, he still was not satisfied because he felt that the race of heroes, the Narts, still needed something else to ensure their well-being and survival. So he went to the wise Lady Satanaya, who advised him to set off about the world to see how other peoples lived, to search to the very edge of the earth itself, and perhaps by that means fulfil his quest.

Tlepsh returned to his smithy, fashioned a pair of boots from his strongest steel, put a heavy torque about his neck and a hat upon his head, took up his walking staff, and set off upon his quest. He travelled through an immense forest for one whole year. He leapt a crag and a river and then bounded over seven

more rivers, until he came to the shore of a great sea. There he
fashioned a raft for himself from the branches of three nearby
trees. Upon reaching the other side, he found a group of
attractive young women enjoying themselves there on the sand.
Not being one to waste such an opportunity, he tried to chat
them up, but it soon became clear that they weren't the least bit
interested in him. This had never happened to him before and he
wondered what kind of women they were. They told him that
they were the followers of a goddess, Lady Tree, and taking pity
on him, they took him to meet their mistress so that his honour
might be restored.

When he came into the hall of Lady Tree he was confronted by
a fabulous being, neither fully human nor fully tree: her trunk
was mighty; her hair reached like clouds up into the heavens;
and her roots sank down deep into the earth. Not only that, but
she had the most beautiful eyes he had ever seen too. Strewn all
about her were fabulous treasures. She bid him welcome and
prepared a feast for him, then she said:

"How did you travel so far? You're the first mere man who
has ever managed to reach me."

"I'm no mere man," Tlepsh replied, "Actually, I'm one of the
gods."

One thing led to another, Lady Tree was clearly attracted to
him, and they ended up spending the night together. Afterwards,
despite gaining the love of this fabulous creature, Tlepsh was
still not content and the need he felt to fulfil his quest for the
Narts was, if anything, even stronger than it had been before.

"I'm sorry but I must leave you, Lady Tree," he said. "I have
to find what it is that the Narts still need, even if I must travel to
the very edge of the earth itself for it."

Lady Tree was distraught when she heard this.

"Stay and be my beloved", she begged him. "My hair reaches
up into the heavens, so that I know all the stars and I shall give
to you also knowledge of them. My roots reach deep down into

the earth, so that I know all the life that springs from there, and I shall place in your arms all this life. My trunk stands in the world, so that I know the earth has no edge and I shall give to you all the treasure that is on the surface of the earth."

But nothing she could say or do would change his mind, and so he set off once again. Tlepsh, to cut a long story short, travelled vast distances but without success, and in the end had to abandon his quest. Defeated he returned to Lady Tree.

"Welcome, Tlepsh," she said, "And what have you learned from your travels then?"

"I've learned that the earth has no edge," he replied.

"Yes, and what else?"

"That the human body is harder than the hardest steel."

"Yes, and what else?"

"That the hardest road is the one travelled alone."

"Yes, and what else? That life is beautiful perhaps?"

"Yes, Lady Tree, life is beautiful, but it's of no importance to me and can never be if I can't find what it is the Narts need to survive."

"Your Narts," she replied, "they're arrogant and stubborn, and one day this will be the death of them. But if you'd stayed, you'd have found what you needed here, from me," and with this she placed in his arms a baby sun. "This is our child. Now, return to the Narts."

He returned to the Narts and pointed to the sky.

"Do you see the Milky Way above?"

"We do," they answered.

"Then follow it at nights when you go out on raids, and follow it home when you return. That way you'll never get lost. But, this baby sun above must be cared for and nurtured. Who's going to volunteer to do that then?"

Seven women stepped forward and said,

"We'll nurse and care for him. We certainly don't want any harm to come to him, especially if it would put our own men in danger of getting lost."

But, in time, despite their ministrations, the baby sun (as babies do) wandered off to play, became lost and vanished. At first the women searched for him, but when they could not find him they ran to the men. The Narts mounted their horses and set off to find him, but they too were unable to find any trace of him. Then in desperation they turned to Tlepsh.

"Tlepsh! The Milky Way has wandered off and we can't find him. Go to his mother, Lady Tree, because he's probably returned there to play."

Tlepsh did as they had asked, but when he came into the presence of Lady Tree and asked her if the baby sun had returned to her she said,

"Our child's not here. There's nothing to be done, except for you to turn back. Perhaps he'll return and the Narts will prosper or perhaps he'll be lost forever and the Narts will perish."

And so, with a heavy heart, Tlepsh returned to the Narts.

* * *

The worship or veneration of trees was at one time widespread across Eurasia. The Norse had the world-tree, Yggdrasil; the Kelts had their druids and sacred oaks and groves; the Romans had a special link between their supreme god, Jupiter, and the oak; the Greeks had sacred groves, one of their gods, Dionysios, had a tree incarnation, and there is evidence for local tree goddess cults; the nomadic Iranians of Classical Antiquity, who roamed the steppes of Central Asia and the Ukraine, have left a burial at Pazyryk in Siberia, which shows a goddess on a throne holding a tree while a horseman pays homage to her; in India a pole festooned with flowers and ornaments, called "Indra's Tree", is the centre of a round dance; this Indic tree has a clear parallel in the European practice of dancing around the Maypole, which must have been a tree originally; tree images abound in early Mesopotamian art and of course the Bible itself makes good use of trees; and in the Caucasus the Abkhazians, kinsmen of the Circassians, have sacred trees and groves.

... Both the Circassian and Norse trees are cosmic in their grasp: their branches both lead up to heaven, encompassing the stars; their trunks both occupy the world of man; and their roots both extend downward into the subterranean realms. Yggdrasil, the Norse tree, means ygg 'terrible' and drasil 'steed', and was taken to be an incarnation of the horse of the Norse supreme god, Odin, which he rode upon his exploits. Thus, the trees of both traditions are intimately associated with raids. In the Circassian myth these raids are nocturnal and are illumined by the child of the tree, the Milky Way. Tlepsh himself bears some similarities with Odin, who is closely associated with Yggdrasil in a number of ways. Both gods have large hats, both make use of walking sticks, and both travel vast distances in short times (taken from http://www.circassianworld.com/colarusso_3.html [accessed 18/08/09]).

In shamanism the tree is one of the means used to access other realities. The Upper World can be reached by climbing its trunk and the Lower World by travelling down through its roots. It expresses the sacrality of the world, its fertility and perenniality. It is related to the ideas of creation, fecundity, and initiation, and finally to the idea of absolute reality and immortality, representing the universe in continual regeneration.

The story that follows comes from Armenia, one of the neighbouring countries to Georgia. Armenia is the smallest of the former Soviet republics, and is bounded by Georgia in the north, Azerbaijan in the east, Iran in the south, and Turkey in the west. Frequently referred to as one of the cradles of civilization, it is also considered by many to have been the first country in the world to officially embrace Christianity as its religion (c. 300).

The Fire Horse

There was once upon a time an old man who had three sons: two of them were clever, but the third was stupid and dirty. Day and night this stupid fellow idled about the house and did nothing. Now the father had sowed a piece of land, and the seed had sprung up well and was already in the ear. But every night someone came and damaged the crop. In order to put a stop to that, the father said to his sons: "dear children, take it in turns to go at night to the field; watch it and try to catch the thief."

The first night the eldest son went out. But about midnight sleep overpowered him and he nodded off. In the morning he went home and said: "I did not close my eyes all night. I got as stiff as a piece of wood with the cold, but I saw nothing of the thief." The next night the second son went out, slept the whole night, and told the same story when he went home. The third night it was the turn of the stupid son. He took a rope with him, sat down at the edge of the field and waited. As it came near to midnight he felt sleep overpowering him, and he took out his knife, cut his finger and rubbed salt in the wound. So his sleep passed off. But exactly at midnight the ground suddenly shook, a wind rose, and a horse came flying right down from heaven with wings of fire and let itself down on the field. Clouds came out of its nostrils and lightning flashed from its eyes. And the horse began to eat the corn, but trampled down more than it ate.

The stupid son crept slowly up to the horse, sprang suddenly upon it, and threw the rope round its neck. The horse pulled with all its might, shied and stamped, but could not tear itself loose. The stupid son held it fast. When at last it grew tired of struggling it tried pleading instead: "John, little friend, let me go, I will do you great service if you only let me loose."

"Good," said John, "but how shall I find you again?"

"When you want me come out to the field, whistle three times and call: 'Fire-horse, Fire-horse! Come quickly,' and I will be with you at once." John let the horse go and bade him leave the field alone from that time forward.

Then he went home.

"What have you seen? What have you done?" his brothers asked him.

"I saw a fire-horse. I caught it and made it promise me that it would leave our field in peace." He did not tell them the rest, and the brothers laughed heartily at their stupid brother, but from that day on the field was left alone.

A day or two later the king sent messengers to every town and village in his kingdom to make this announcement: "Lords, citizens, nobles and peasants! Our mighty king is about to hold a feast and invites you all to attend it. The festivities will last for three days. Take your best horses with you. The king's only daughter, who is more beautiful than the sun, will sit on the balcony of a tower. Whoever can jump so high on his horse that he can reach the princess and pull her ring from her finger, to him the king will give his daughter to wife."

John's brothers went off to the feast, not to try their own luck, but just to look on. John begged them to take him with them. "Why take you stupid?" they asked, "do you want to frighten the people with your ugly face? Stay at home."

So the brothers mounted their horses and set out. But John went to the field and called his fire-horse. Where did it come from, that in a moment it stood before him? John jumped over its head, after which his face was quite changed; he had become such a handsome fellow that no one would have believed he was stupid, dirty John.

Then he mounted his horse and hastened to the feast. There he saw that a huge crowd had collected on the wide square before the king's palace. And on the balcony of the high tower the king's daughter sat, as beautiful as the moon, her ring gleaming like the sun. No one was bold enough to venture the spring up into the air. But who was this who lifted his hand? Our John! He gripped his horse firmly with his knees, the animal neighed and made a tremendous spring, which was short only by three steps. The people bit their tongues and wondered. But John turned his horse round and fled. On the way he met his brothers; as they did not get out of his way fast enough he gave them a tremendous blow as he passed and disappeared. When he got home to his field, he jumped off and at once became stupid John again. He let the horse loose and went home. In the evening his brothers returned and told their father with bated breath all that had happened. But John only listened to them and laughed to himself.

Next day the two elder brothers went again to the festival, and again they refused to take their youngest brother with them. John went to the field, called his fire-horse, jumped on its back and rode away. As he came near the king's palace, he saw there was an even bigger crowd than on the previous day. Everyone was looking at the king's daughter, but no one dared to attempt to spring. John again gripped his horse with his knees and let it go. This time it failed by only two steps. The people were still more astonished. John disappeared more quickly even then before, and gave his brothers an even heavier blow as he passed them …

On the third day he came again. But this time he gave his horse such a blow with his whip … That the animal leapt with extraordinary power into the air and reached the balcony. John pulled the ring off the finger of the princess and turned round to ride away. "Hullo, there! Stop him! Stop him!" everyone shouted, the king, the queen, and all the people … But he was already away.

John came home and bound up his hand with a rag. "What has happened to your hand?" the women of the house asked him. "I pricked it picking berries. It is nothing," answered John, and stretched himself out before the fire.

The brothers soon came home and told their father what had happened in the town. In the meantime John wanted to have a look at his ring, but hardly had he got the rag off when the whole hut began to shine. "Stupid! Don't play with fire," his brothers shouted at him; you are no use for anything, and you nearly set the house on fire just now. You should have been sent away long ago."

Three days later messengers came again and commanded all the people of the country to come to a new festival which the king was about to hold. Whosoever did not come would have his head cut off.

What could be done in that case? The father went with his whole family to the festival. They ate, drank, and made merry. At the end of the banquet the princess herself handed round honey-water. John got some too. And that day he looked like someone I would not like you to have even for an enemy – in torn clothes, with dirty, untidy hair he stood there, and round his hand he had a dirty rag; he was a loathsome spectacle. "Youth, why is your hand bound up?" asked the princess; "let me see what is wrong."

John took off the bandage, and on his finger gleamed and sparkled the princess's ring. She pulled it off his finger, led John to her father, and said: "Father, this is my bridegroom."

John was then taken to the bath, washed, combed, anointed, dressed in other garments, and he looked such a handsome youth that his own people hardly knew him again.

Then the wedding was celebrated and the festivities lasted for seven days and seven nights.

Taken from *Caucasian Folk-tales*: Selected and Translated from the originals by Adolf Dirr. Translated into English by Lucy Menzies. 1925 London & Toronto J.M. Dent & Sons Ltd.

* * *

Again and again in stories "*...we see how things appear in threes: how things have to happen three times, how the hero is given three wishes; how Cinderella goes to the ball three times; how the hero or the heroine is the third of three children*" (Booker, 2004, p.229). Look at what we have in this particular tale, for example:

- There was once upon a time an old man who had three sons
- "When you want me come out to the field, whistle three times and call: 'Fire-horse, Fire-horse! Come quickly,' and I will be with you at once."
- The festivities will last for three days.
- He gripped his horse firmly with his knees, the animal neighed and made a tremendous spring, which was short only by three steps.
- On the third day he came again
- Three days later messengers came again

But why does the triad, a group or series consisting of three items, feature over and over again in folktales and legends, wherever they may originate from? The answer is that it has long been of significance for a number of reasons. Three is linked with the phases of the moon (waxing, full and waning), and with time (past, present and future). Pythagoras even went as far as to call three the perfect number, in that it represents the beginning, the middle and the end, and he thus regarded it as a symbol of Deity. The triad is also the basis of *The Threefold Law* (a.k.a. the *Law of Return*) in the *Wiccan Rede*, an ethical code for witches, which adds a reward for those who follow the code, and a punishment for those who violate it. The law states that "All good that a person does to another returns three fold in this life; harm is also returned three fold." And that is presumably what the main hero and the villains of this story, namely his two cruel brothers, have to look forward to.

As for the ending of the story, it is basically of the "happily ever after" variety: "Then the wedding was celebrated and the festivities lasted for seven days and seven nights." Like the importance of the triad, already referred to, the heptad features prominently in many folk-tales too. The Heptad, a group or series consisting of seven items, has long been of significance for all sorts of reasons. Consider the human body, for example:

The body has seven obvious parts – the head, chest, abdomen, two legs and two arms. There are seven internal organs – stomach, liver, heart, lungs, spleen and two kidneys. The ruling part, the head, has seven parts for external use – two eyes, two ears, two nostrils and a mouth. There are seven inflections of the voice – the acute, grave, circumflex, rough, smooth, the long and the short sounds. The hand makes seven motions – up and down, to the right and left, before and behind, and circular. There are seven evacuations – tears from the eyes, mucus of the nostrils, the saliva, the semen, two excretions and the perspiration. (We could also add that it is in the seventh month the human offspring becomes viable and that menstruation tends to occur in series of four times seven days).

Seven is a mystic or sacred number in many different traditions. Among the Babylonians and Egyptians, there were believed to be seven planets, and the alchemists recognized seven planets too. In the Old Testament there are seven days in creation, and for the Hebrews every seventh year was Sabbatical too. There are seven virtues, seven sins, seven ages in the life of man, the Seven Wonders of the World, and the number seven repeatedly occurs in the Apocalypse as well. The Muslims talk of there being seven heavens, with the seventh being formed of divine light that is beyond the power of words to describe, and the Kabbalists also believe there are seven heavens – each arising above the other, with the seventh being the abode of God (Berman, 2008a, p.122).

Moreover, the seven days and seven nights of the wedding festivities is by no means the only reference to the number seven that can be found in Armenian folklore. In the Yazidi belief system, the world is now in the care of a Heptad of seven Holy Beings, known as angels or heft sirr (the Seven Mysteries). Additionally, the number also features in an Armenian spring festival that was held until recent times. Young women, in great secrecy, would go up onto the mountain to cut Haurot and Maurot flowers (species of hyacinth). "In the meantime, others, who were hiding from the first group, drew water from seven springs or rivers. In the evening, the flowers and the water were poured together into a basin called Hagvir. The liquor which resulted was a potion for happiness" (Bonnefoy, 1993, p.266).

Although the cosmology described in Creation Myths will vary from culture to culture, the structure of the whole cosmos is in fact frequently symbolized by the number seven, made up of the four directions, the centre, the zenith in heaven, and the nadir in the underworld. In other words, the essential axes of this structure are the four cardinal points and a central vertical axis passing through their point of intersection that connects the Upper World, the Middle World and the Lower World. As for the names by which the central vertical axis that connects the three worlds is referred to, these include the world pole, the tree of life, the sacred mountain, the central house pole, and Jacob's ladder.

Many other reasons for the importance of the heptad can be listed as well:

- Among the Hebrews oaths were confirmed by seven witnesses or by seven victims offered in sacrifice (cf. the covenant between Abraham and Abimelech with seven lambs, *Genesis*, chap. xxi. vv. 28, 21–28). The Persian Sun God, Mithras, had the number seven sacred to him too.

- The highest beings in Zoroastrianism, the Amshaspands, are also seven in number: Ormuzd, source of life; Bahman, the king of this world; Ardibehest, fire producer; Shahrivar, the former of metals; Spandarmat, queen of the earth (the Gnostic Sophia); Khordad, the ruler of times and seasons and Amerdad, ruling over the vegetable world.

- Sanskrit lore has very frequent references to the number seven too: *Sapta Rishi,* seven sages; *Sapta Kula,* seven castes; *Sapta Loka,* seven worlds; *Sapta Para,* seven cities; *Sapta Dwipa,* seven holy islands; *Sapta Arania,* seven deserts; *Sapta Parna,* seven human principles; *Sapta Samudra,* seven holy seas and *Sapta Vruksha,* seven holy trees.

- The Assyrian Tablets also teem with groups of sevens: seven gods of sky; seven gods of earth; seven gods of fiery spheres; seven gods maleficent; seven phantoms; spirits of seven heavens and spirits of seven earths.

- The Moon passes through stages of seven days in increase, full, decrease, and renewal, and there are the seven stars in the head of Taurus called the Pleiades.

- The Kabalists describe seven classes of Angels: Ishim, Arelim, Chashmalim, Melakim, Auphanim, Seraphim and Kerubim. The Judaic Hell was given seven names by the Kabalists too: Sheol, Abaddon, Tihahion, Bar Shacheth, Tzelmuth, Shaari Muth and Gehinnom.

- Other heptads can be added to those above too. The seven prophetesses in the *Old Testament* are Sarah, Miriam, Deborah, Hannah, Abigail, Huldah and Esther. The seven Catholic Deadly Sins are pride, covetousness, lust, anger, gluttony, envy and sloth. The seven Gifts of the Holy Spirit (*Isaiah* xi. v. 2) are wisdom, understanding, counsel, fortitude, knowledge, piety and fear of the Lord. The seven

Champions of Christendom were St. George for England, St. Denis of France, St. James of Spain, St. Andrew of Scotland, St. David of Wales, St. Patrick of Ireland and St. Antonio of Italy.

- We can also add the historic city of Rome to the list, which was built upon Seven Hills; the Palatine, Cœlian, Aventine, Viminal, Quirinal, Esquiline and the Capitol (adapted from *The Heptad* in Westcott, 1911, pp. 72-84).

- Last but not least, mention should be made of what have been described as the seven basic plots (see Booker, 2004), and the suggestion that all the stories that have ever been written are based on these. The seven basic plot types Christopher Booker identifies are overcoming the monster, rags to riches, the quest, voyage and return, comedy, tragedy and rebirth.

Prior to their conversion to Christianity, the principal god of Armenia was Aramazd, whom the Armenians called "the Architect of the Universe, Creator of Heaven and Earth." He was also the father of the other gods. The Armenians annually celebrated the festival of this god on the 1st day of Navasard, 1 when they sacrificed white animals of various kinds – goats, horses, mules, with whose blood they filled goblets of gold and silver. The most prominent sanctuaries of Aramazd were in the ancient city of Ani in Daranali, the burial-place of the Armenian kings, as well as in the village of Bagavan in Bagravand.

The son of Aramazd was Mihr, Fire. He guided the heroes in battle and conferred wreaths on the victors. The word mehian ("temple") is derived from Mihr; also some Christian names. One of the months in the ancient Armenian calendar (Mehekan) was named after him. His commemoration-day was celebrated with great splendour at the beginning of spring. Fires were kindled in the open market-place in his honour, and a lantern lighted from one of these fires was kept burning in his temple throughout the year. This custom of kindling fires in the spring is still observed in some parts of Armenia, and a nineteenth-century account of the festival by Abeghian is described by Boetticer:

On the afternoon of the 13th of February, [the 13th of February according to the old style calendar corresponds to the 26th of February of the Latin calendar] which is the day before the church festival of the purification, a pile of wood consisting usually of thorn-wood, cane, and straw is gathered together in the churchyard. The entire community comes together in the church on the night of the same day, each person provided with a candle. After the vespers all stand about the pile of shrub and wood, the newly married during the year making the first row. The candles are lighted from the church light, and after the priest has blessed the pile, it is set ablaze from all sides, after which the candles are put out. As soon as the fire has died down, the candles are re-lighted from the glowing embers which are regarded as sacred, and carried home where they are used to light a pile of shrub and wood that has been gathered on the roof of the house. The young people jump over the fire while the young women and married women march around it saying, "May it not itch me, and may I not receive any scabs," taking care just to singe the border of their dresses. The ashes, as well as the half-burned woodstuffs are preserved, or scattered in the four corners of the barn, over the fields or in the garden, for the ashes and flames of the firebrands are believed to protect people and cattle from sickness and the fruit trees from worms and caterpillars. In the homes of the newly married the festival is celebrated with music and dance, the young couples especially making it a point to dance about the sacred flames, while in some places special food is prepared in honour of the occasion.

Various prophesies are made during the festival, for example, if the flame and smoke blows to the east, it is a sign of a good harvest for the coming year, if toward the west, a bad growth is expected (Boetticer, 1920, pp.57-58).

Although the Persians and the Armenians were both worshippers of Mihr, the conceptions and observances of the two nations differed. The Armenian sacred fire was invisible, but the Persian was material and was kept up in all the temples. For this reason the Armenians called the Persians fire-worshippers. But the Armenians had also a visible fire-god, who, although material, was intangible – the sun – to which many temples were dedicated and after which one of the months (Areg) was named.

Long after the introduction of Christianity, there was a sect of sun-worshippers existent in Armenia, who were called "Children of the Sun." A small remnant of them is still supposed to be found, dwelling between the Tigris and the Euphrates. Traces of sun-worship are also evident in the Armenian language and in the Armenian literature of Christian times. Some sayings and phrases are still in use which contain references to sun-worship, such as the expression of endearment, "Let me die for your sun!" and the oath, "Let the sun of my son be witness."

One of the most famous Armenian goddesses was Anahit – the Being of Golden Birth, who answered to the Greek Artemis and the Roman Diana. She was a "pure and spotless goddess," and, as a daughter of Aramazd, was "mother of chastity," as well as the benefactress of the whole human race; "through her the Armenian land exists, from her it draws its life; she is the glory of our nation and its protectress"; and for her the ancient Armenians felt intense love and adoration.

As for the importance of the horse in this story, it is worth noting what Eliade has to say on the association between the animal and the shaman's drum, and the way in which the drum has traditionally been used in a number of cultures by shamans to induce the trancelike state required for journeying:

The iconography of the drums is dominated by the symbolism of the ecstatic journey, that is, by journeys that imply a breakthrough in plane and hence a "Center of the World." The drumming at the beginning of the séance, intended to summon the spirits and "shut them up" in the shaman's drum, constitutes the preliminaries for the ecstatic journey. This is why the drum is called the "shaman's horse" (Yakut, Buryat). The Altaic drum bears a representation of a horse; when the shaman drums, he is believed to go to the sky on his horse. Among the Buryat, too, the drum made with a horse's hide represents that animal (Eliade, 1989, p.173).

According to Yakut beliefs, the horse is of divine origin. In the beginning God is said to have created a horse from which a half-horse, half-man descended, and from this being humankind was born. The Sky-Horse deity, Uordakh-Djesegei, plays a major role in Yakut religion, and Yakut mythology depicts many other scenes in which deities and guardian spirits descend to the earth as horses. The honorable goddess Ajjyst, the patron of child-bearing, appears as a white mare, as does the goddess called Lajahsit. The horse is of great significance to the shaman too. "A Yakut shaman's healing performance is unthinkable without a horse, just as the entire ceremony cannot occur without the shaman's participation ... A horse, its image, or at times, an object personifying the animal is always present in the shaman's preparations and performances" (Diachenko, 1994, p.266).

Among Turkic-speaking people of South Siberia, including Tuvinians, the horse can play an important role too, and it is the drum that can represent the animal ridden by shamans to travel to other worlds. Its handle can be regarded as the horse's "spine; the plaits of leather attached to the upper part of the ring symbolize the reins of the horse; the drumstick is a lash, which beats a drum only in certain places" (Diakonova, 1994, p.253).

Whether he is chosen by gods or spirits to be their mouthpiece, or is predisposed to this function by physical defects, or has a heredity that is equivalent to a magico-religious vocation, the medicine man stands apart from the world of the profane precisely because he has more direct relations with the sacred and manipulates its manifestations more effectively. Infirmity, nervous disorder, spontaneous vocation, or heredity are so many external signs of a "choice," an "election." Sometimes these signs are physical (an innate or acquired infirmity); sometimes an accident, even of the commonest type, is involved (e.g., falling from a tree or being bitten by a snake); ordinarily ... election is announced by an unusual accident or event – lightning, apparition, dream, and so on (Eliade, 1989, pp.31.32).

It has been proposed that, "Every wonder tale is rich in the use of magic and must have some task for its hero to accomplish ...various physical qualities enable the hero to overcome great obstacles. Frequently, he is aided by superhuman companions in fulfilling tasks. These helpers have great prowess in running, throwing, eating, hearing, drinking, and lifting." (Hoogasian-Villa, 1966, p.69).

In The Fire-horse it is the horse itself that fulfils this role by being able to sprig high enough for the youngest brother to reach the princess's ring. There is a problem, however, with the term "wonder tale" as it fails to fully acknowledge the probable origin of the kind of story we are considering here, the way in which it more than likely dates back to pre-Christian times, and it is for this reason the term "shamanic story" is to be preferred. Such a story can be defined as one that has either been based on or inspired by a shamanic journey, or one that contains a number of the elements typical of such a journey.

Characteristic of the genre is the way in which the stories tend to contain embedded texts (often the account of the shamanic journey itself), how the number of actors is clearly limited as one would expect in subjective accounts of what can be regarded as inner journeys, and how the stories tend to be used for healing purposes.

The shamanic journey frequently involves passing through some kind of gateway. As Eliade explains, the "clashing of rocks," the "dancing reeds," the gates in the shape of jaws, the "two razor-edged restless mountains," the "two clashing icebergs," the "active door," the "revolving barrier," the door made of the two halves of the eagle's beak, and many more – all these are images used in myths and sagas to suggest the insurmountable difficulties of passage to the Other World [and sometimes the passage back too] (Eliade, 2003, pp.64-65).

In The Fire-horse reaching the balcony of the tower is the gateway the youngest brother is required to gain access to. It is also frequently the case that to make such a journey requires a change in one's mode of being, entering a transcendent state, which makes it possible to attain the world of spirit. Sometimes when we are faced with overwhelming difficulties, we find an inner strength we never knew we had, and perhaps this helps to explain how our hero attains the necessary state that enables him to achieve his goal. It has been suggested that the purpose of the descent, "as universally exemplified in the myth of the hero is to show that only in the region of danger ... can one find the 'treasure hard to attain' " (Jung, 1968, pp.335-336) and this is borne out by what transpires in the tale. For although our hero is initially unable to reach the princess, he refuses to be deterred by his failures and so springs again into the unknown in order to achieve his goal, in the same way that Carlos Castaneda had to make such a leap of faith into the abyss at the end of his semi-autobiographical novel *Tales of Power* (1974). What we can see from this is that for shamanic work to be effective, being able to trust in the process is imperative.

It can be argued that perhaps the defining characteristic and main attribute of the shaman has traditionally been his or her mastery of the ability to journey at will to other realities to intercede with the spirits on behalf of clients and to bring back information to help them with their dilemmas, thus working to restore balance to the community. What we find by the end of the tale is that the youngest brother has had his own balance restored as a result of his initiatory journey, and will thus be better able to help others with their problems in future. In other words, he has become a "wounded healer".

The person traditionally chosen to be the shaman of a community was often a wounded healer – someone who had been through a near-death experience and who was consequently well-suited to helping others through difficult times in their lives. The experience would establish the healer's warrant to minister to his people's needs as one who knew how to control disorder. The profession to which the concept of the wounded healer most aptly applies today is probably that of the psychoanalyst and the kind of shamanism that has been practised by tribal peoples through the ages can thus be viewed as a form of pre-scientific psychotherapy (see Lewis, 2003, p.172).

So what we find is that The Fire-horse includes all the elements one would expect it to do as a typical example of its genre – a hero who does not really fit in (in this case due to his perceived stupidity and the fact that he is shunned by other members of his community), a hero who is able to understand the language of the animals and communicate with them, a spirit helper in the form of the Fire-horse, a journey into non-ordinary reality that entails facing barriers that have to be crossed and quests that have to be accomplished, "shape-shifting" (of the hero from an ugly into a handsome man), and finally the restoration of the equilibrium of the community. This is brought about as a result of the presumably successful consummation of the marriage between the two young people. All this indicates that what we have here is essentially a shamanic story rather than what at first sight might appear to be just a simple fairy tale, and the same can be seen to be the case in other stories included in this collection too.

References

Berman, M. (2007). *The Nature of Shamanism and the Shamanic Story:* Newcastle: Cambridge Scholars Publishing.

Berman, M. (2008) *The Shamanic Themes in Armenian Folktales,* Newcastle upon Tyne: Cambridge Scholars Publishing.

Berman, M. (2010) *Shamanic Journeys through the Caucasus,* California: Pendraig Publishing.

Blavatsky, H.P. (1980). "The Number Seven." In *Theosophist,* June, 1880.

Boettiger, L.A. (1920) *Armenian Legends and Festivals,* Minneapolis: University of Minnesota ww.archive.org/stream/ armenianlegendsf00boet/armenianlegendsf00boet_djvu.txt [accessed 12/08/2009]).

Booker, C. (2004) *The Seven Basic Plots*: *Why we tell Stories,* London: Continuum.

Boyajian, Z. C. (comp.) (1916), Armenian Legends and Poems, New York: Columbia University Press (Scanned at sacred-texts.com, June 2006. Proofed and Formatted by John Bruno Hare. This text is in the public domain in the United States because it was published prior to January 1st, 1923. These files may be used for any non-commercial purpose, provided this notice of attribution is left intact in all copies).

Castaneda, C. (1974). *Tales of Power.* New York: Simon and Schuster.

Diachenko, V. (1994). "The Horse in Yakut Shamanism." In Seaman, G. & Day, J.S., *Ancient Traditions: Shamanism in Central Asia and the Americas.* Boulder, Colorado: University Press of Colorado.

Diakonova, V.P. (1994). "Shamans in Traditional Tuvinian Society." In Seaman, G. & Day, J.S., *Ancient Traditions: Shamanism in Central Asia and the Americas.* Boulder, Colorado: University Press of Colorado. Menzies, London & Toronto: J.M. Dent & Sons Ltd.

Eliade, M. (1989). *Shamanism: Archaic techniques of ecstasy.*

London: Arkana (first published in the USA by Pantheon Books 1964).

Eliade, M. (2003). *Rites and Symbols of Initiation*. Putnam, Connecticut: Spring Publications (originally published by Harper Bros., New York, 1958).

Hoogasian-Villa, S. (1966). *100 Armenian Tales*. Detroit, Michigan Wayne State University Press.

Jung, C.G. (1977). *The Symbolic Life*. London and Henley: Routledge & Keegan Paul.

Lewis, I.M. (2003). *Ecstatic Religion: a study of shamanism and spirit possession,*

3rd Edition. London: Routledge (first published 1971 by Penguin Books).

Westcott, W.W. (1911) (3rd Edition) *Numbers, Their Occult Power and Mystic Virtues*, London, Benares: Theosophical Pub. Society. Scanned, proofed and formatted at sacred-texts.com, August 2009, by John Bruno Hare. This text is in the public domain in the US because it was published prior to 1923.

Czaplicka, M.A. (2007) *Shamanism in Siberia*: [Excerpts from] *Aboriginal Siberia: A Study in Social Anthropology*, Charleston SC: BiblioBazaar (Original Copyright 1914, Oxford).

Kaeter, M. (2004) *The Caucasus Republics*, New York: Facts on File Inc.

Kharitonova, V. (1999) *Spelling-conjuring art of the East Slavs: Problems of traditional interpretations and possibilities of modern research.* Moscow, Russia: Institute of Ethnology and Anthropology of Russian Academy of Sciences.

Koghbatsi Yeznik (1994) *Refutation of Heresies*. Yerevan, Armenia: Yerevan State University. (In Ancient Armenian)

Kurkjian, V.M. (1958) A History of Armenia, published by the Armenian General Benevolent Union of America. The text is in the public domain. http://penelope.uchicago.edu/Thayer/E/Gazetteer/Places/Asia/Armenia/_Texts/KURARM/home.html [accessed 13/08/09].

A tall tale is a story with unbelievable elements, related as if it were true and factual, and the final tale in this section, which comes from Mingrelia on the eastern shore of the Black Sea, provides the perfect example of one.

Polyphemus is the gigantic one-eyed son of Poseidon and Thoosa in Greek mythology, one of the Cyclopes. His name means "much spoken of" or "famous" and he plays a pivotal role in Homer's *Odyssey*. In Book 9, Odysseus lands on the Island of the Cyclopes during his journey home from the Trojan War. He takes with him twelve men to find food and drink, and they eventually find a large cave, which is the home of the great Cyclops Polyphemus. When Polyphemus returns home with his flocks and finds Odysseus and his men, he blocks the cave entrance with a great stone, trapping the remaining Greeks inside. Polyphemus then crushes and immediately devours two of his men for his meal.

The next morning, Polyphemus kills and eats two more of Odysseus' men for his breakfast and exits the cave to graze his sheep. The desperate Odysseus devises a clever escape plan. He spots a massive unseasoned olivewood club that Polyphemus left behind the previous night and, with the help of his men, sharpens the narrow end to a fine point. He hardens the stake over a flame and hides it from sight. That night, Polyphemus returns from herding his flock of sheep. He sits down and kills two more of Odysseus' men, bringing the death toll to six. At that point, Odysseus offers Polyphemus the strong and undiluted wine given to him by Maron. The wine makes Polyphemus drunk and unwary. When Polyphemus asks for Odysseus' name, promising him a guest-gift if he answers, Odysseus tells him "οὖτις," literally "nobody." Being drunk, Polyphemus thinks of it as a real name and says that he will eat "nobody" last and that this shall be his guest-gift – a vicious insult both to the tradition of hospitality and to Odysseus. With that, Polyphemus crashes to the floor and passes out. Odysseus, with the help of his men, lifts the flaming stake, charges forward and drives it into Polyphemus' eye, blinding him. Polyphemus yells for help from his fellow Cyclopes that "nobody" has hurt him, but they just think Polyphemus is making a fool out of them or that it must be a matter with the gods, and they grumble and go away.

In the morning, Odysseus and his men tie themselves to the undersides of Polyphemus' sheep. When the blind Cyclops lets the sheep out to graze, he feels their backs to ensure the men aren't riding out, but because of Odysseus' plan, he does not feel the men underneath. Odysseus leaves last, riding beneath the belly of the biggest ram, and Polyphemus doesn't realize that the men are no longer in his cave until the sheep and the men are safely out.

Some tall tales are exaggerations of actual events, for example fish stories ('the fish that got away') such as, "that fish was so big, why I tell you, it nearly sank the boat when I pulled it in!" Other tall tales are completely fictional tales set in a familiar setting. Tall tales are often told so as to make the narrator seem to have been a part of the story. They are usually humorous or good-natured. The line between myth and tall tale is distinguished primarily by age; many myths exaggerate the exploits of their heroes, but in tall tales the exaggeration looms large, to the extent of becoming the whole of the story.

This particular variant of the Polyphemus Saga is also very much an illustration of how one story invariably leads into another, and so reflects what storytelling is really all about.

A Polyphemus Saga: A Mingrelian Variant

A dark, wet night once overtook a traveller on the road between Redut-Kale and Anaklia (on the eastern shore of the Black Sea). In the midst of a wood, far from any human habitation, a herd of wolves surrounded him and tried to drag him off his horse. The horse stopped dead and could not be made to go on either by persuasions or threats. What good was it to the traveller that he had tied little sticks to the tail of his horse?* The wolves tried to seize him in spite of that. Cold terror seized the poor man, his sword hung useless in his hand. There remained only one thing for him to do, to cry for help as loud and long as his lungs could serve him. Then a light appeared in the distance, the wolves disappeared, and the horse galloped towards the light. It was a torch held by a man who lived in the one little house of that district, who had hastened out when he heard the cry for help. The traveller warmed himself in the hut and then told his host what had happened to him. But his host had a far more dreadful story to tell.

"Brother," said he, "you think you are unfortunate because the creatures there in the wood attacked you. No, if you only knew what I have to bear in my heart, you would be thankful that nothing worse happened to you. You will notice that we all wear mourning here. We were seven brothers, all fishermen. We often stayed out in our ship for months at a time, and only sent in a boat once a week with the fish. But one day we noticed, just as we had thrown out our nets, that our ship was being carried away from land – something was drawing her away and we could not stop her. So she sailed on and on and on; after some weeks we saw a rocky shore before us, from which a river of honey flowed.

"Our ship was pulled right up to this honey stream. As we got quite near it an enormous fish came up underneath our ship, its jaws over a fathom broad. He swallowed the honey with such greed that the stream was almost dried up. That was the biggest of all fish; he swam to this place to eat the honey, but in Anaklia he ate maize. It seemed that our nets had caught in his fins, and that was how he dragged us with him. Now while he was eating the honey, we quietly cut through the net which attached us to him. The fish swam away and we were left behind. But we did not know where we were. We laughed with delight at seeing land again, but we wept with anxiety as to our fate.

"Then we took counsel as to what was to be done. We agreed to load up the ship with honey and wax from the stream, and then to follow along the shore always in the same direction. We loaded honey for a whole week, and on the day before we were to sail we saw that a flock of sheep and goats were approaching the honey-stream. The shepherd was a giant and one-eyed. He held a stick as thick as a pillar in his hand, and he twirled it round like a spindle. A dreadful fear took hold of us. The giant pulled our ship ashore and drove us with his hand to a great building which stood in the midst of a wood. The trees were so high that one could not see the tops of them. Even the rushes were as high and as thick as oak-trees are with us.

"The gigantic building itself was formed of enormous blocks of undressed stone, and was divided up inside into several different divisions for the different kinds of animals: the goats, the sheep, the lambs and the kids each had their own divisions. The one-eyed giant locked us in and then drove away his herd. We tried to break open the door, but in vain. Like mice in a mouse-trap, we ran round and round and up and down from morning till night. In the evening our one-eyed giant came back, locked up his animals and lighted a fire. He laid whole trunks of trees upon it. Then he took a roasting-spit, fetched himself a fat sheep and roasted it, without preparing it in any way. Nay, he even did not kill it, but stuck it living on the spit. The beast struggled in the flames till its eyes burst. The giant ate up the whole sheep, lay down and began to snore. Next morning he ate two more sheep, but in the evening he took the fattest of us brothers, stuck him on the spit and began to roast him. Our brother struggled dreadfully, and screamed for help. But what could we do? When our brother's eyes burst, the one-eyed giant tore off one of his legs and threw it to us, the rest he ate up himself. We buried the leg. On the following days it was the turn of my other brothers; finally only my youngest brother and myself were left. We were almost mad with fear and horror, and longed for death – no such dreadful death after all. Now when he had eaten the fifth brother and lay snoring at the fire, we two stole quietly up to the roasting-spit which he had stuck into the ground beside him and pulled it out with great difficulty. We put it into the fire and waited in fear and trembling till it became red-hot. Then we thrust the red-hot spit into his one eye. The blinded giant sprang up with such fury in his pain that we thought he would break through the roof, but he only made a great wound in his head. With dreadful screams he rushed through the whole building, trampling sheep and goats to death under his great feet. But he could not find us because we always slipped through between his legs. Next morning the animals began to make a noise because they wanted to go out to the meadow. The giant opened the door, stood in front of it and let the sheep and goats pass singly through between his legs, feeling the back, the head and the body of each. He did that till midday; then he got tired of it and contented himself with touching the back of each creature as it passed through. Happily, my brother had still a knife. We skinned two sheep with it, covered ourselves with the skins and determined to creep through between his legs. Half dead with fright, I tried my luck first. The giant noticed nothing. I was outside. My brother followed. We went at once to our ship, which lay still at the same spot. Our hopes of saving our lives increased. In the meantime the herd of the one-eyed giant came along. We picked out the finest animals and took them with us on to the ship. But hardly had we cut the anchor rope, when the giant appeared and felt for our ship. When we were out of his reach, we called out our names to him that he might know who had played such an evil game with him. Full of rage he sent his blows thrashing after us; so heavy were they that the sea foamed up and our vessel nearly went to the bottom. After making many false starts in various directions, and after many privations, we arrived home at last."

*The Mingelians considered that a good way to protect themselves from wolves was to bind a few little sticks to the tails of their horses.

Have you noticed how the one thing people are always doing about the wind is complaining? They complain about the wind blowing rain into their faces, blowing their umbrellas inside out, spoiling their new hairdos, chilling their bones, causing a draught, blowing their newspapers away or their candles out etc., etc. The one thing they never seem to do is to acknowledge, how without it, life as we know it would probably cease to exist. The following tale touches on this subject, and reminds us of the folly of taking what we have been blessed with for granted:

The Tribute of Roses – A Legend

In our most blessed and favoured country, where the sun shines so brightly, where the flowers have such a sweet, sweet fragrance, where the birds sing so melodiously, long ago in bygone times, when neither I nor my father nor my forefathers had been born, there lived a young and splendid couple in the Aule of Mokde [Note of the Translator: Aule is the common term for a very small village or rather mountain hamlet in the Caucasus.] They were always most hospitable and everybody praised them, but the Lord, who always delights in seeing the religious and the poor well-treated, fully rewarded them and abundantly furnished them with rich presents, thus clearly showing them his appreciation for their good deeds. They had everything that could be desired: youth, beauty, good health, riches, and reputation, they sincerely loved one another and their inner happiness was as great as their outer appearance and great success. Their children were healthy, clever, good and lovely to look at. Their elder son, little Timitch, distinguished himself especially through his strength and ability; he was endowed with most fiery eyes, once sparkling like flashes of lightning, then again as soft and innocent as the eyes of a young mountain goat.

For nine years the happy husband and wife lived thus, when suddenly between the aules of Mokde and Khamki a very bloody strife ensued and led to much destruction of life and property. During this strife, when the father of Timitch was mercilessly killed as well as his brothers and sisters, while the mother was taken prisoner and led off as a captive, Timitch himself was saved by some inexplicable wonder and soon became the favourite and greatest pride of the whole aule. In the meantime his mother, who was still a beautiful and youthful woman [in our country the women can be married at the early age of twelve] was sold and taken away to Turkey, where her wonderful appearance was the chief ornament of the Sultan's harem. In this select collection of beautiful and highly attractive women, her good looks and sweet disposition cast a dark shadow over all the rest – just as our bright sun dims all other planets.

The Sultan got perfectly wild with delight over her, and he incessantly showered most precious weavings, gorgeous carpets and splendid stones of one colour and priceless shawls – in a word everything that the rich, rich East could produce lay at her graceful feet. Nevertheless in the midst of all these flatteries and endless temptations she always remained faithful to her husband. It needed a marvellous mind and character like hers, while utterly refusing to fulfil the wishes of the Sultan, to still remain the governess of his heart and the immediate object of his kind and thoughtful attention. In these proceedings a lucky circumstance firmly assisted her – viz., the fact that she had been preparing herself to become a mother already four months before, when she happened to be taken prisoner. The loving and enchanted Sultan decided to patiently await the birth of the baby, which was foreign to him, and then marry his unusual captive, who was of royal blood and thus fully had the right to be an empress. The nearer she approached the time when a child should be born, the gayer the future Sultana became, so that those surrounding her really imagined that she had forgotten her husband. But oh, how terribly mistaken they were! Indeed, the eventful day came and a daughter Tousholi was born.

When they brought her the baby she long looked at it and tears came in floods out of her magnificent eyes, afterwards she made the sign of the cross on it and gave orders that it should be carried off.

"Call Samson to me," she said. Samson was the eunuch, given and attached to her personal service by the Sultan and who had faithfully done his duty by her side. She knew how to win his esteem and confidence, especially as he was himself a Christian (of course quite secretly). When he arrived she ordered him to take up the opakalo (probably a kind of Eastern fan) and protect her, while sleeping, from uncomfortable and noisy flies; but she did not want to sleep – this was simply a sly device to make everybody leave her apartment and get out. She profited by this occasion to tell Samson the following facts:

"Samson, to thee I trust the new-born daughter Tousholi, promise me if possible secretly to make a Christian of her, as sincere and earnest in her belief as thou thyself. Among all these unbelievers thou wert not a slave to me, but a true and faithful friend and a tender and thoughtful brother. By the almighty mercifulness of God I am destined to live not much longer, for I hope to-day already to be able to unite myself with my dear husband, while thee I ask to take the place of this dear orphan's parents. Thou knowest my whole history, my strength does not enable me to speak to thee as freely as I should like. For the sake of the outward appearance I shall leave Tousholi nominally to the care of the Sultan, and I am convinced that at first everything will go right with you. When, however, your situation changes, I hope indeed that you may find means to return to Mokde and look up my first-born child, whose natural obligation it is to be the powerful protector of his defenceless sister and her very aged educator, but now give me my little kindjall (Caucasian dagger) – fear nothing, I shall not cut myself open, for I have not even the strength to do that."

Samson placed in her now feeble hands the handsomely ornamented little kindjall, artistically decorated with precious stones and fastened to a most gorgeous girdle. This was the wedding present of her husband and she never left it out of her sight. The submissive old man, through his tears beheld how the face of the sick woman suddenly lit up and how, her eyes flashing with some extraordinary fire, she bravely pulled the little kindjall out of the sheath and put its thin blade, which was as sharp as the tongue of a snake, up to her lovely mouth.

"She sincerely kisses it," thought Samson, and quieted

himself; but the precious little kindjall had yet another resemblance with the tongue of a snake, of which the faithful servant knew nothing. It was indeed poisoned!

Having heroically swallowed the deadly poison, the sick woman commanded Samson to instantly inform the Sultan that she desired to see him. The all-powerful adorer of this Christian heroine immediately made his appearance and was utterly distressed when he saw the signs of approaching death already marked on her magnificent features. In his anger against those standing about, he threatened them with perfectly atrocious punishment if they did not that moment find doctors able to bring his favourite back to life. In the meantime with a weak but expressive and comprehensible movement of her hand, the patient showed that she desired to be left alone with him. All the rest disappeared in a second and she broke out thus:

"My minutes are counted, I am dying, not paying you back in any way for your innumerable marks of kindness to me, and nevertheless I wish to ask yet another favour of you: be a father to my new-born daughter! It is my firm and irrevocable wish that my true and ever-faithful Samson shall stay by her and bring her up in none but my own dear religion; when, however, you are tired of her, simply send them to Mokde to my son Timitch, and even if he be no longer living, I am fully convinced that the excellent daughter of my loving husband will always find protectors and friends among the good and kindly inhabitants of Mokde." With these serene words she breathed her last breath. The tremendous fury and utter despair of the Sultan went beyond any description. The court body-doctor and the arifa (i.e., the lady who administrates the harem) were hung without delay, but Samson and his sweet little pupil were given very fine and expensive apartments with magnificent board.

Every ten days the old man was obliged to bring little Tousholi to the Sultan, who having tenderly caressed her and given riches to the faithful servant, let them retire, giving the strictest orders that those who surrounded them should never hinder, trouble, or disturb them in any way. Thus three long years easily went by. The childish features of the face of Tousholi now acquired a most striking resemblance with the marvellously beautiful features of her late mother. The courtiers began to notice repeatedly that the Sultan after a time had fallen in love with her, was earnestly reflecting about something and frequently sighing. Thus the visits, which used to last but a few minutes, now became very long indeed, while little Tousholi, with her childish caresses, gained the affection of the Sultan more and more. Immediately two parties sprang up: the first, wishing to make Tousholi their excellent instrument in order to get the upper hand and overrule the Sultan, and thus naturally, constantly and unceasingly chanting her praises and flattering her to the skies; the second, which had resolved to make her perish and from this reason never letting one occasion go by without trying to snap at her and pull her down from her exalted position.

During the fearful struggle of these two desperate parties, Tousholi's childhood went by and she was already a grown-up maiden, when the kind-hearted Sultan died. His successor by chance belonged to the dangerous and inimical party, and so the sharp and careful Samson began to energetically demand to be allowed to go away to Mokde. The permission to start for the home journey was given with great joy and satisfaction, and very soon they had already arrived at Mokde. Here there was no difficulty in finding out Timitch. He was known by young and old alike. The old servant silently took from Tousholi's baggage that precious girdle with the kindjall, which he had handed to her mother just a few hours before her untimely death and passed it to Timitch, drawing his attention to a splendid all-sparkling round tablet. On it were inscribed the dear names of his glorious parents.

"This is the remarkable girdle which was always around the waist of my all-beloved mother!" cried out the youth.

"Well, say now I prythee where is she staying? How can I possibly reward thee – oh, thou grand old man? Art thou sent by her?"

"I verily came to this memorable village by her sacred will," reverently answered Samson. "While dying she ordered me to lead thy sister to thee and hand her over to thy mighty care and protection."

"What, my sister? Well, well, is it possible that not all sisters and brothers perished together with their splendid father?"

Saying this he closely looked at the young girl and was evidently struck and impressed by her perfectly unusual beauty.

"The resemblance with your mother ought to be sufficient to convince you of the truth of my words."

Afterwards innumerable questions and answers were mutually exchanged. The old man and Tousholi settled down in the house of Timitch and Samson heartily rejoiced, seeing soon how the youngsters became friends. But nevertheless there was nothing to rejoice about! The twenty-year-old Timitch, fiery, not given to reflections, unaccustomed to restrain himself in any way, was entertaining such intentions as would make Samson's hair stand on end if he thoroughly understood their meaning. What is there strange in the fact that the twelve-year-old Tousholi was unable to guess at the thoughts of her brother and firmly trusted him in everything with all her simple childish sincerity of soul. The passionate attraction of Timitch grew not with days, but with hours, and once during a promenade, without being at all disturbed by the presence of grave old Samson, he actually went as far as to tell her of his peculiar intentions.

Samson, astonished and disapproving the plan, threw himself in between the young people and was stupefied when seeing a dagger pointed towards him, but the terrified Tousholi speedily hid herself near a precipice. Seeing the immediate danger, the dying faithful Samson cursed the wicked and lawless boy, and lo! suddenly a great wonder took place.

Timitch was transformed into a wind and began to crazily blow and whistle over the precipice, but the submissive and ever loyal servant was turned into a gigantic rose bush, in the midst of which a rose of unusual size was growing and constantly blooming. By the will of God, angels with marvellous, all-glorious singing slowly let themselves down into the precipice, majestically lifted out from it the magnificent body of Tousholi and carefully placed it in the very centre of the superb rose, the all-fragrant leaves of which gradually closed up and thus buried inside of them the deceased. Attracted by the all-glorious angelic singing, the faithful inhabitants of Mokde ran together in crowds to the rose and many of them clearly saw how the angels grace-fully interred Tousholi in the rose. But Timitch could by no means quiet down; with anger and greatest passion he threw himself upon the rose bush and wished to break it down, but the more he shook the lovely branches, the closer and firmer did they stick to the rose and the better did they defend her from his unjustified attacks and depredations. When, however, he finally succeeded in carrying off the tender, tender leaves of the rose, Tousholi was no more to be seen, for her body had completely evaporated in the marvellous fragrance.

The religious inhabitants of Mokde enclosed the beloved holy rose with a very massive stone wall, called this spot Tousholi, and yearly when the first beautiful rose came out they celebrated a fête, which has quite a character of its own and is popularly known as "the tribute of roses."

The ceremony consists of the following points: Every young girl gathers a tremendous full bunch of rose leaves and standing one behind the other, they await the exit of the very oldest man in the village. He comes out, dressed in a white suit and bearing in his hand a white flag, the point of which is richly decorated with roses and covered with sweet little bells, while at the end a large wax candle burns. Putting himself at the head of the procession, the old man gives a solemn signal and the procession duly and martially directs itself towards Tousholi; behind it at a considerable distance followed young people, leading sheep and bringing along with them the customary offerings, i.e., horns, balls, hatchets, silks, etc. The procession winds around Tousholi three times with beautiful singing in which is described in detail all that we have mentioned above – then the girls in their turn enter through the great fence and put down in a certain place their splendid fragrant offerings, softly adding:

"Saint Tousholi, help and assist me! Holy Samson, shield and protect me from the cursed Timitch and all of that kind!"

On the top of a pretty mound, formed by the magnificent rose leaves, the old man solemnly fixes his standard, saying: "Saint Tousholi, make me wise, Holy Samson, help me to guard and defend all these tender maids from the cursed and all-hated Timitch and all those who follow his wicked example!"

After this earnest speech the old man sits down at the foot of the graceful flag, while at his own feet the young girls settle down. Then the young people enter the enclosure and kneeling on one knee pronounce a most reverential greeting discourse to the hermit and the maidens and then they turn about and face an opposite corner, where they curse Timitch who hath wickedly cast a dark shadow over their beloved aule; afterwards they cut up the sheep and gaily feast with all those present. When I was but a very small boy I happened to be in this place and was favoured with seeing with my own eyes one or two roses inside the enclosure, which it appears is existing even in our advanced and enlightened days. These roses are really unusually large in size, but nevertheless neither a grown-up girl nor even a new-born youngster can possibly find place inside the flower. I under-stand that at that time they used to say with regret, that the fête of "the tribute of roses" did not repeat itself yearly! Thus little by little ancient customs disappear and antique amusements are superseded by new ones, which are not always successfully chosen; only grim Timitch never changes, for he is quite as restless now as ever before, here moves and weeps like a child, there makes a row, yes rebels like a robber and lawlessly destroys whole buildings. His dislike for roses never ceases, and as soon as he sees a sweet little flower he immediately begins to blow around it with impatience and anger until he hath scattered the beautifully fragrant leaves far and wide over the country. Now the story of Tousholi is already forgotten, but her name, among the Chechenzes, is given to all such interesting places, where they go to make sacrifices and fervently pray.

* * *

Taken from The Project Gutenberg EBook of *Caucasian Legends*, by A. Goulbat. Translated from the Russian of A. Goulbat By Sergei de Wesselitsky-Bojidarovitch, Hinds, Noble & Eldredge West Fifteenth St. New York City.

This eBook is for the use of anyone anywhere at no cost and with almost no restrictions whatsoever. You may copy it, give it away or re-use it under the terms of the Project Gutenberg License included with this eBook or online at www.gutenberg.org Produced by Jeroen Hellingman and the Online Distributed Proofreading Team at http://www.pgdp.net for Project Gutenberg (This file was produced from images generously made available by The Internet Archive/American Libraries.)

Many teaching stories come from Sufi sources and are about a character called Mullah Nasr-udin (the most commonly found spelling of the Mullah's name). Although a number of different nations claim the Mullah as their own, like all mythological characters he belongs to everyone. The Mullah is a wise fool and his stories have many meanings on multiple levels of reality. The stories show that things are not always as they appear and often logic fails us.

How the Mulla Nasr-eddin discovered a New Illness

There happened to be a particularly cold winter one year. The Mulla Nasr-eddin loved warmth, but in his saklya [mountain hut] the wind was blowing from all directions and there was no firewood. Then the Mulla lay down in his bed and covered himself with all the warm things that were in the house.

He lay there for one day, he lay for two; in fact, he lay there for a week. Not having seen him for some time, his fellow-villagers got worried and started asking the Mulla's wife what the matter was. But his wife did not answer them so they decided to go and call on the Mulla to find out for themselves.

When they entered the *saklya* and saw that the Mulla was lying underneath three fur-coats and several sheepskins, they exclaimed, "What's wrong with you, Mulla Nasr-eddin? Are you ill?"

"Ill!" The Mulla Nasr-eddin answered form under the fur-coats, in a voice barely audible, and with teeth chattering.

"Just what illness do you have then?" The neighbours asked.

"Winter", answered the Mulla, even more quietly. And then they finally realized what the problem was.

* * *

Adapted from *The Pranks and Misadventures of the Mulla Nasr-eddin* compiled by Roman Fatuyev, originally published by Ordzhonikidze Regional Publishing House, Pyatigorsk, 1937, translated from the Russina by D.G.Hunt.

The final tale in this section is all about journeying on currents of air into the Upper World, three brothers born on earth but who live in the sky, and it starts with a formulaic opening sentence, which is the Georgian equivalent of our *Once upon a time*:

Ivane the Dawn

There was and there was not, what could there have been, better than God himself? There was a smith who lived in a certain town. He had no children, though he longed to have them with all his heart.

Once, his wife went to fetch water from the nearby spring. As soon as she put her jug into the stream, she saw three red apples floating around close to her. The smith's wife grabbed the apples and took them home. She ate one of them, gave one to her husband, and they shared the third one between them.

After eating the apples, the wife became pregnant. Nine months passed by and one evening the baby cried from his mother's stomach:

"Go and fetch the priest to christen me as soon as I am born, as I will fly up into the sky the minute I am born."

And so, just as it was getting dark, a baby boy was born. He was christened straight away and called Ivane the Twilight, as he was born at dusk. The baby sucked at his mother's breast and flew up into the sky. The priest was getting ready to leave but suddenly another child called from its mother's stomach:

"Don't let the priest go yet because I will be born at midnight."

And so, in the middle of the night, another boy was born. The priest christened him and called him Ivane the Midnight according to the time of his birth. Like his elder brother, he also sucked at his mother's breast and afterwards, flew up into the sky.

Once again, just when the priest was getting ready to leave, they heard another unborn baby cry:

"Don't let the priest go yet because I will be born at dawn."

And so, another boy was born at dawn and, just like his brothers, he was christened straight away and called Ivane the Dawn.

Since that day, the three brothers have lived in the sky. They flew in and out of the clouds and among the stars in the sky but they never got to know one another. Of course, they flew back to their mum to be breast fed, but they did not see each other in their own home either. This was because Ivane the Twilight flew home at dusk, Ivane the Midnight in the middle of the night, and as for Ivan the Dawn, he came to visit his mum at sunrise. However, as soon as they felt full, they flew back into the sky once more.

Time passed and the boys grew into lads. They no longer needed their mother's milk and so did not return to their home every day anymore. They would fly back once each week, take enough food to last them for a week and then fly back to their clouds and stars.

Now it just so happened that the king of the country had a throne and a palace in the same town where the smith and his wife lived. The king had three beautiful daughters who were scared of getting burnt by the sun or of catching a cold and so never left the comfort and safety of their cosy rooms in the palace whatever the weather was like.

One day their father told the princesses:

"My dear daughters, it is not good enough to sit inside the palace day and night. Just for once, go out, see the country and enjoy the sunshine."

The daughters followed their father's advice and went out for a walk into the garden of the palace. It was in the afternoon. All of a sudden, the sky clouded over, a terrible storm broke, and before the girls realized what was happening, a Devi with nine heads flew down from the sky, kidnapped all three of the princesses and disappeared back up into the clouds again

This dreadfully sad news spread all over the town and made everyone very sad. The king sent the people to all four corners of the world to look for his daughters, but in vain! Then the midwife, who had helped the smith's wife to give birth to her three sons, went to the king and told him:

"In this town there lives a certain smith and he has three sons who live in the sky. They can fly like birds and rule the sky as well as the earth. These boys must know where your daughters are better than anybody in this world!" And so the midwife advised the king to ask the boys about his daughters.

The king organized a feast for the very same evening and sent his servants to invite the smith's sons to it, amongst other subjects of his. The boys, of course, were not at home, but their mother promised to send them to the king's palace as soon as they came home.

First came Ivane the Twilight, as soon as it got dark. His mother laid the table for him as usual, and when he was ready to go, she said:

"Please, stay home tonight. The king is organizing a feast and you are invited."

The son obeyed his mother and stayed at home. She made a bed for him and he fell fast asleep as soon as his head hit the pillow. In the middle of the night it was Ivane the Midnight's turn to come home. His mother met him as usual and after he had had his supper, she said:

"Don't go back tonight, my son. Our king is organizing a feast and if you didn't go there he'd be very hurt."

So Ivane the Midnight obeyed his mother. When she took him to another room and he saw some unknown man sleeping in the bed, he was furious and asked her:

"Who is this man sleeping here?"

"That is your elder brother. He was born in the same night as you but as you both come at different times, you have not yet met each other before."

Ivane the Midnight calmed down then and fell asleep next to his brother. At dawn it was time for Ivane the Dawn to arrive and his mother met him the same way as she had met his brothers, told him what the king wanted and showed him his brothers.

Ivane the Dawn lay down next to his brothers and fell fast asleep too.

At dawn, when Ivane the Twilight woke up, Ivane the Midnight had been asleep since midnight and Ivane the Dawn had just fallen asleep. Ivane the Twilight had not met his brothers yet and he was furious to see two strangers in his house. He jumped up from his bed and grabbed hold of his sword. At this moment the boys' mother entered the room and seeing Ivan the Twilight with the sword in his hand, she became most upset and cried out fearfully:

"Why do you need the sword? Who do you see here to be your adversary?"

"Who are these strangers if not my foes then?"

"Oh, no, no!" cried his mother sorrowfully, "these are your twin brothers. Like you, they also live in the sky. Last night they came home and I asked them to stay."

After some time, Ivane the Midnight and Ivane the Dawn woke up and all of the brothers embraced each other lovingly. Then they went to the king's palace where the king met them with great respect. After the feast, the king then asked the brothers if they had heard anything about his daughters.

Both Ivane the Twilight and Ivane the Midnight replied that they had heard nothing of the princesses. But the youngest brother, Ivane the Dawn, stood up and said this to the King:

"Your Majesty, one day, I was lying on a fluffy cloud, having a rest while observing the sky and the clouds at play with each other. Suddenly, I heard weeping and wailing. I looked behind and what did I see? One huge Devi, holding three distraught-looking girls flew past. I wanted to shoot an arrow but then changed my mind as I didn't want to harm the girls. If I'd killed the Devi, he'd have fallen on the earth and the girls would have died as well. Since then I haven't seen or heard anything of them though."

The king was delighted to have found at least one man who

had seen his daughters since that sinister day, and this is what he said to Ivane the Dawn:

"If you three brothers manage to find my daughters and save them from captivity, I will marry them to you. The eldest brother will marry my eldest daughter, the middle one my middle daughter and the youngest daughter, who is more beautiful than the sun herself, will become your wife, Ivane the Dawn."

Ivane the Dawn agreed and the brothers went to look for the princesses. After a long, long walk they approached one huge rocky mountain. This mountain was so huge that it stretched from one sea to another with one foot in each. In addition to this, it was so high that it was impossible for a man to see its top. At the foot of this mountain there was a camp and a huge iron man was sleeping in it.

Ivane the Dawn sent his brothers in the tent to wake the iron man up, but they were not able to move his fingers. Then Ivane the Dawn entered the tent on his own, hit the man with his bow and then the man did wake up! Seeing Ivane the Dawn towering over him, the iron man was scared and asked him to have mercy on him and, in return, he would help him as a brother would.

Ivane the Dawn agreed, but on one condition. He asked the iron man to help them climb the mountain. The iron man replied:

"If you can make a long iron chain, we could throw it up the mountain and then use it to pull ourselves up."

"No problem – I'm a blacksmith's son so of course, I know how to make something like that" replied Ivane the Dawn, and went to fetch some iron. After a while he brought a lot of iron back with him, and all the tools blacksmiths use except for an anvil.

"Don't worry about that!" said the iron man. "You can use my head as an anvil." And he knelt down and lowered his huge iron head on to the earth for the purpose.

Ivane the Dawn and his brothers made a very, very long iron chain, with which they reckoned they could reach the top of the mountain in a day. After that, the brothers planned to hook the chain on to a huge rock to hold it securely, and to use the big steel forks on the other end to hook it on the top of the mountain. Ivane the Dawn asked his brothers to help him try and hurl the chain up to the top of the mountain, but even the three of them together were not able to lift it up from the ground whereas the iron man managed to toss the chain up to the middle of the mountain for them.

"Now, look at me," said Ivane the Dawn, emboldened by their success up to this point. This time, all by himself, he took one end of the chain, hurled it up to the top of the mountain and hooked the forks on to it securely. Once again, Ivane the Dawn asked his brothers to climb up the chain, but although they made a start, they were just too scared and returned back down to the middle again. Then it was the iron man's turn to try, but just as he was approaching the top of the mountain, he accidentally looked down, and when he saw how high up he really was, he got so frightened that he could hardly even crawl down the chain back to the others.

Ivane the Dawn asked his brothers to look after the iron man till he returned and then, with courage he never knew he had before, ran up the chain to the top of the mountain like an ermine to look for the princesses.

After a long walk he came to a palace made out of copper. This palace belonged to a Devi with seven heads and he was married to the eldest princess. Ivane the Dawn entered the palace and saw the eldest princess there. She told him the whole story of what had happened to her and her sisters and then, added sorrowfully:

"Although of course I'm grateful for all your efforts, I wish in a way that you hadn't come because the Devi will eat you and I pity you for this."

"Don't worry, the Devi and I will sort out this problem somehow" he replied, trying to reassure her.

"If you kill that horrible Devi, I will marry you" said the

woman.

"I might kill him" replied Ivane the Dawn, "but I cannot promise to marry you. Who knows though – you may become my sister-in-law one day."

Having said this, Ivane the Dawn left the palace and lay down in the shade, waiting for the Devi to return.

In the evening, the Devi with seven heads arrived. He was riding his horse and not aware of any threat at all. When the horse came closer to the palace, it was startled by something and suddenly pulled up. The Devi scolded his stallion:

"May you get eaten by a wolf! What is the matter with you? Have you seen Ivane the Dawn?"

And then, when the Devi entered the gates of his palace, the first person he saw was Ivane the Dawn!

"Ivane the Dawn, have you come as a friend or as a foe?" The Devi shouted.

"As a foe, of course! How can I be your friend?" replied Ivane the Dawn.

At this, the Devi dismounted from his horse and angrily issued the following challenge:

"If you've come as a foe, blow on the earth now!"

"I'm not the only person here. If you think you're so powerful, you blow!" replied Ivane the Dawn defiantly.

The Devi blew on the earth and turned it into copper, but it did not help him. Ivane the Dawn planted him into the earth up to his knees at the very first attempt. Next, the Devi wrestled with Ivane the Dawn and did exactly the same thing to him. At the second attempt, Ivane managed to plant the Devi up to his waist in the earth and cut off three of his heads. The Devi was furious. He got hold of Ivane the Dawn and planted him up to his waist in the earth too. Ivane the Dawn then jumped up, took hold of the Devi, planted him into the earth up to his neck and cut off the remaining heads. Next, he entered the palace again, said goodbye to the eldest princess, asked her to wait for him, and took the princess's engagement ring with him for his eldest brother.

After this, Ivane the Dawn continued on his way in search of the younger princesses. After a long, long walk he came to another palace, made out of silver this time. This palace was owned by a Devi with nine heads and he had the middle princess as a wife. Ivane the Dawn entered the palace fearlessly and found that only the hostess was at home. When the princess learnt who the guest was and why he had come she implored Ivane the Dawn to give up his plan as she was sure her husband the Devi would kill him. Ivane the Dawn calmed her down, and lay down in the shade, waiting for the Devi to return.

In the evening, when the Devi with nine heads was approaching the palace, he sensed from his horse's behaviour that something was upsetting him, and the Devi scolded the stallion:

"You stupid horse! What are you frightened of? You're not going to meet Ivane the Dawn here!"

And then, when the Devi entered the gates of his palace, the first person he saw was Ivane the Dawn!

"Ivane the Dawn, have you come as a friend or as a foe?" The Devi shouted.

"As a foe, of course! How can I be your friend?" replied Ivane the Dawn.

At this, the Devi dismounted from his horse and angrily issued the following challenge:

"If you've come as a foe, blow on the earth now!"

"I'm not the only person here. If you think you're so powerful, you blow!" replied Ivane the Dawn just as defiantly as he had done before his earlier encounter, and then they started wrestling.

Likewise, just as he had done in his previous encounter, Ivane the Dawn planted the Devi into the earth at the third attempt and once again cut off all its heads. Next, he entered the palace made out of silver, took the engagement ring for his middle brother and asked the princess not to leave the palace until he returned. After this, he went in search of the youngest princess.

An exceedingly long walk followed, until Ivane the Dawn eventually came to the palace which belonged to the Devi with twelve heads – the one where the most beautiful princess lived. The palace and its surroundings were made of pure gold and everything sparkled and shone in the sunlight. Ivane entered the palace, embraced his intended wife-to-be and told her all he had gone through. But when he explained he had come to kill the Devi with twelve heads and to take her away with him to be his bride, the princess started to cry:

"Don't even try to meet the Devi, he is the strongest in the world and there is no one to beat him."

"Fear not!" replied Ivane the Dawn, fearlessly, "I know exactly how to deal with him."

Having done his best to calm her down and reassure her that everything would be all right, Ivane the Dawn left the palace and lay down in the shade to wait for the Devi's return. In the evening, the Devi came home from hunting, but just as he was approaching the palace his horse stumbled and then pulled up for some reason.

"Go on, you stupid thing!" shouted the Devi to his horse, whipping it "What is scaring you? Even if Ivane the Dawn is lurking around here somewhere, I will cut him up into small pieces and throw them to the ravens to eat."

Cursing and swearing, the Devi came into the yard, and found Ivane the Dawn waiting for him there.

"Ivane the Dawn, have you come as a friend or as a foe?" The Devi shouted.

"As a foe, of course! How can I be your friend?" replied Ivane the Dawn.

At this, the Devi dismounted from his horse and angrily issued the following challenge:

"If you've come as a foe, blow on the earth now!"

"I'm not the only person here. If you think you're so powerful, you blow!" replied Ivane the Dawn just as defiantly as he had done before his two previous encounters.

The Devi blew and the earth all around turned into gold. Then the Devi and Ivane went for each other and started to fight. The earth quaked and huge trees were blown down, the grass was trampled upon and even the clouds in the sky started to quiver and tremble like the leaves on the trees. Both, the Devi and Ivane the Dawn were very strong and initially neither of them could gain the upper hand. The Devi even planted Ivane into the earth up to his waist, but Ivane somehow managed to pull himself out of the earth, rushed at the Devi, swung him around and, before he knew it, the Devi this time found himself in the earth, up to his shoulders. Ivane the Dawn drew his sword and cut off nine heads out of the twelve. The Devi was exhausted and had had enough.

"How do people fight in your world then?" he asked Ivane the Dawn.

"In my country, when people are tired of fighting, they just have a little rest and then renew the battle" he replied.

"Good! Let me have a little rest then," asked the Devi.

Ivane the Dawn thought about it for a while but then decided against it. He sliced off the three remaining heads, took his bride-to-be, and both of them got ready for the journey back home.

Just as they were about to leave though, the princess made the following observation:

"Ivane the Dawn, look behind. There's a lot of gold around, isn't there? Why should we leave it all here?"

"Devis do not have gold," replied Ivane. "Your husband cheated you to make you love him for his riches. Look – let me show you." He blew at the gold palace and the yard and suddenly, everything turned into dust. In exactly the same way, the copper and silver palaces were turned into dust and vanished too. Afterwards, Ivane took the princesses and all of them travelled back to the huge rocky mountain together.

First, Ivane the Dawn let the eldest of the three princesses climb down the chain and shouted to Ivane the Dusk to look after her. Next, he let the middle princess make the descent and shouted down to his brother, Ivane the Midnight, to take care of her. Finally, it was the turn of the youngest princess, but she told Ivane she felt that the iron man was going to betray them, and implored Ivane to go first instead. Ivane the Dawn refused though, saying he could not possibly leave her behind. But as soon as the princess had climbed down the chain, the iron man cut the chain into two, leaving Ivane the Dawn stranded on the top of the mountain. What could he do? Just then, he heard his fiancee's voice calling him from the foot of the mountain:

"Ivane the Dawn, the Devi had a stallion and it will help you! It's in the middle of the sea, tied to a huge rock. The Devi took him and left him there as it would not obey him. Go there and fetch the stallion!"

So Ivane the Dawn went there and found the stallion, which was so exhausted from being kept without food that it could hardly move.

The stallion asked Ivane the Dawn to let him go to the Black Mountain for three days to restore his strength and to have a little rest. On the fourth day, he brought it back, groomed and harnessed it. However, when he tried to mount him, the stallion hesitated and asked Ivane to let him rest for one more night. Ivane the Dawn agreed and next morning, as the stallion had promised, it was ready to carry and serve Ivane the Dawn. As soon as Ivane mounted the stallion, it flew high up into the sky and reached the town two days before the princesses, his brothers and the iron man.

Now Ivane the Dawn did not want anybody to know that he was in the town until his brothers, the princesses and the iron man arrived. So the stallion suggested he take his armour and clothes back to the Black Mountain and offered to leave three hairs from his tail behind. When Ivane the Dawn needed him, all he had to do was to burn the hairs and the stallion would appear in a second. Ivane the Dawn followed his advice, let the horse go, and then he put on shabby clothes and went into the town centre to find a job until the others arrived. He went in the end to the town's goldsmith and asked him to let him work as his apprentice.

The goldsmith agreed to take him on, and as he was making an axe at the time, he asked Ivane the Dawn to help him. Ivane the Dawn took the huge hammer and hit the anvil with it, and such was his power that the anvil disappeared into the ground. This took the goldsmith by surprise as he had never met such as strong man in his life before.

After two days the iron man and the brothers reached the town with the kidnapped princesses. The king was beside himself with happiness and made all the arrangements and preparations for the weddings. Normal practice was to celebrate the eldest daughter's wedding first, next the wedding of the middle daughter, and finally it would be the turn of the youngest princess' wedding. However, it happened that the two elder daughters did not have the rings – they were with Ivane the Dawn – and according to local custom, it was necessary for all three of the princesses to have identical engagement rings.

So the youngest daughter gave her engagement ring to the servant, who was then sent to all the goldsmiths of the town. The goldsmiths were asked to make two rings identical to the one of the youngest princess. However, they all refused to do so. Finally, the man came to the goldsmith Ivane the Dawn worked for, who, like all the others, wanted to say no. But Ivane the Dawn whispered into his ear "take the ring and I will help you to make them," and so he agreed to take on the job.

That night the goldsmith went to bed, but Ivane the Dawn stayed on in the workshop, pretending to work on the rings. Next, he took out the oldest princess' ring, wrapped it in a cloth and put it on the shelf. In the morning as soon as the goldsmith entered the workshop, he asked Ivane the Dawn what he had been doing all night long. Ivane showed him the ring and promised that he would make the other ring the next night. The ring was taken to the palace and given to the eldest princess who was so happy that she invited the goldsmith to the wedding. The goldsmith asked Ivane the Dawn to accompany him but he refused to go .As soon as the goldsmith left the house, Ivane the Dawn burnt the hair of his stallion, and before he even had time to draw a single breath, the horse was there by his side.

"What is happening? Is there anything wrong, and what can I do for you?" it asked Ivane the Dawn.

Ivane the Dawn put on his clothes followed by his armour, mounted the stallion, and this is what he told him:

"Fly high please, and when my eldest brother and his wife have left the church, take me as close as you can because I want to give him a slap that he won't forget for what he has done."

The stallion did as he was told to. He flew high up to the sky and as soon as the newly-weds came out from the church, the stallion plummeted and Ivan the Dawn slapped his eldest brother as strongly as he could. Next, Ivane the Dawn sent the stallion back to the Black Mountain with his clothes and armour and returned home clad in rags.

When the drunken goldsmith came back from the wedding, he told his apprentice what he had seen in the wedding: how the stallion had appeared from the sky, how the rider had slapped the groom, frightened the guests and then disappeared again. Of course, being drunk, he exaggerated a lot.

"In that case, it's a good job that I didn't come to the wedding. I would have died of fear," muttered Ivane the Dawn in response.

That night Ivane the Dawn stayed in the workshop again and in the morning gave his master another ring. The goldsmith took the ring to the middle princess. The princesses now understood everything. The youngest princess started to cry, wondering whether Ivane the Dawn had come back and, if he had, why he did not rescue her. However, Ivane the Dawn knew when the right time would come. On the day of the middle brother's wedding, he asked his stallion to help him again and both of them flew to the church. And this time Ivane the Dawn slapped his middle brother as hard as he could for what he had done.

In this way, Ivane the Dawn punished his elder brothers and now, the time of the iron man had come. Ivane the Dawn burnt the stallion's hair once again and when the horse appeared, he put on his clothes and armour, and ordered it to fly down to the church before the iron man and the youngest princess had the chance to enter it.

"We will do as you wish" replied the stallion and both of them flew up to the sky. Fearing nothing, the iron man approached the church, bringing the beautiful princess with him. As soon as they reached the entrance, Ivane the Dawn dismounted from the horse, hit the iron man as hard as he possibly could and planted him firmly and very permanently into the ground. Then, he embraced and kissed his fiancée.

Only then did all the people realize who that stranger was and they cried out with delight at the discovery.

Ivane the Dawn married the youngest princess and when the king died, he became the king. And even today, he is still the king, and rules his country so well that not a single two-faced liar or cheat would ever dream of living there.

Sorrow-there, happiness-here,

Bran- there, flour here

* * *

As this particular tale contains so many shamanic elements, in particular what can be regarded as soul flight (by the brothers) and possession (by the Devi) the obvious starting point is to explain what is meant by this.

> The term 'shaman' is a controversial one. Initially employed by early anthropologists to refer to a specific category of magical practitioners from Siberia, the term is now widely used to denote similar practitioners from a variety of cultures around the world. This application of an originally culture-specific term to a more general usage has caused problems with regard to definition, with disagreements among scholars over whether certain features, such as soul flight or possession, or certain types of altered states of consciousness, should or should not be listed among the core characteristics of shamanism (Wilby, 2011, p.252).

As a result, there are as many definitions of shamanism as there are books written on the subject. Here is my version:

A shaman is someone who performs an ecstatic (in a trance state), imitative, or demonstrative ritual of a séance (or a combination of all three), at will (in other words, whenever he or she chooses to do so), in which aid is sought from beings in (what are considered to be) other realities generally for healing purposes or for divination–both for individuals and/or the community.

A shamanic journey is one that generally takes place in a trance state to the sound of a drumbeat, through dancing, or by ingesting psychoactive drugs, in which aid is sought from beings in other realities, generally for healing purposes or for divination. As for a shamanic story, which *Ivane the Dawn* can be regarded as an example of, it can be defined as one that has either been based on or inspired by a shamanic journey, or one that contains a number of the elements typical of such a journey.

For the shaman, the structure of the cosmos is frequently symbolized by the number seven, made up of the four directions, the centre, the zenith in heaven, and the nadir in the underworld.

The essential axes of this structure are the four cardinal points and a central vertical axis passing through their point of intersection that connects the Upper World, the Middle World and the Lower World. The names by which the central vertical axis that connects the three worlds is referred to, include the world pole, the tree of life, the sacred mountain, the central house pole, and Jacob's ladder. So important is this cosmology considered to be that religion itself has been described by Berger (1969) as the enterprise we undertake to establish just such a sacred cosmos.

Different types of shamanic journeys can be undertaken to the Lower World, for example, where contact can be made with Power Animals and to the Upper World where a practitioner can meet his or her Sacred Teacher[1]:

> The starting point for a journey to the Upper World can be a mountain, a treetop, or even a ladder, from which the shaman envisions himself ascending into the sky; "and despite the variety of socio-religious contexts in which it occurs, the ascent always has the same goal–meeting with the Gods or heavenly powers, in order to obtain a blessing (whether a personal consecration, a favour for the community, or the cure of a sick person)" (Eliade, 1958, p.77).

At some stage of the journey the shaman may come up against a kind of barrier that temporarily impedes the ascent. But once this has been successfully negotiated, the Upper World is reached.

In *Ivane the Dawn*, the starting point for the journey to rescue the possessed princesses is a mountain, and the barrier impeding the ascent is the difficulty posed by the need to construct and then raise the chain.

So who is the shaman in this story then? As is frequently the case in such tales, it is the youngest son of three, and the king-to-be. The fact that Ivane the Dawn turns out to be gifted with superhuman strength marks him out as being different in some way, traditionally one of the marks of a shaman. We should also point out that one of the traditional attributes of the shaman is also his or her ability to communicate with the animals, and the horse is frequently the form of transport used by the shaman to access other worlds.

> Pre-eminently the funerary animal and psychopomp, the "horse" is employed by the shaman, in various contexts, as a means of achieving ecstasy, that is, the "coming out of oneself" that makes the mystical journey possible. ... [I]t produces the "break-through in plane," the passage from this world to other worlds (Eliade, 1964, p.467).

The style of storytelling most frequently employed in both shamanic stories and in fairy tales is that of magic realism, in which although "the point of departure is 'realistic' (recognizable events in chronological succession, everyday atmosphere, verisimilitude, characters with more or less predictable psychological reactions), ... soon strange discontinuities or gaps appear in the 'normal,' true-to-life texture of the narrative" (Calinescu, 1978, p.386). In other words, what happens is that our expectations based on our intuitive knowledge of physics are ultimately breached and knocked out. In the case of *Ivane the Dawn*, for example, the discontinuities start to appear when the three sons fly up into the sky to live.

Three sons, three princesses, and three Devi feature in this tale, and the number three is clearly used for a reason. Three is linked with the phases of the moon (waxing, full and waning), and with time (past, present and future). Pythagoras called three the perfect number in that it represented the beginning, the middle and the end, and he thus regarded it as a symbol of Deity. The importance of the number in *Ivane the Dawn* could well be the result of the influence of Christianity and its use of the Trinity, but it also refers to the three stages in the cycle of life and adds to the universality of the story's appeal.

Writing or talking about shamanism has always been problematic as "the subject area resists 'objective' analysis and is sufficiently beyond mainstream research to foil ...writing [or talking] about it in a conventional academic way" (Wallis, 2003, p.13). Shamans have their own ways of describing trance experience. Outsiders

> might call them 'metaphors', but to shamans these metaphors, such as 'death', are real, lived experiences ... 'Metaphor is a problematic term extracted from Western literary discourse which does not do justice to non-Western, non-literary shamanic experiences. In recognizing this limitation, 'metaphor may remain a useful term for explaining alien shamanic experiences in terms understandable to Westerners (Wallis, 2003, p.116).

Perhaps this is why the accounts of memorable shamanic journeys were often turned into folktales, as it was the only way to make them both understandable and acceptable to people not familiar with the landscapes to be found and experiences to be had in such worlds.

"Sceptics will argue that it is impossible to eliminate from analysis the Christian influence on what sources there are available to us, such that we can never be certain in any one case that we are indeed dealing with beliefs that are authentically pagan. This view is now so widely held that we can in justice think of it as the prevailing orthodoxy" (Winterbourne, 2007, p.24). And the same argument could be applied to the attempt to ascertain whether we are dealing with beliefs that are authentically shamanic in *Ivane the Dawn*. Nevertheless, just because a task is difficult is no reason for not attempting it. If it was, then no progress would ever be made in any research that we might be involved in.

"The goal of the psychic journey varies widely, although it

typically involves *therapy* in a very expansive sense of the term – the "healing" of physical, psychological, or sociological problems" (Glosecki, 1989, p.11). And that is what shamanic stories and shamanic journeys are basically all about. In *Ivane the Dawn* the goal is for the hero to restore the equilibrium of the community in which he lives, and for which he then becomes responsible for.

"While it is true that man depends on his gods, the dependence is mutual. The gods also need man, without offerings and sacrifices, they would die" (Durkheim, 2001, p.38). This applies equally well to the Sacred Teachers and Power Animals met by shamanic practitioners on their journeys to other realities. This is why the shaman is required to both respect and honour these Helpers who assist him or else they will desert him.

References

Berger, P. (1973) *The Social Reality of Religion*, Harmondsworth: Penguin

Calinescu, M. (1978) 'The Disguises of Miracle: Notes on Mircea Eliade's Fiction.' In Bryan Rennie (ed.) (2006) *Mircea Eliade: A Critical Reader*, London: Equinox Publishing Ltd.

Durkheim, E. (2001) *The Elementary Forms of Religious Life*, Oxford: Oxford University Press (originally published in 1912).

Eliade, M. (2003) *Rites and Symbols of Initiation*, Putnam, Connecticut: Spring Publications (originally published by Harper Bros., New York, 1958).

Eliade, M. (1964) *Myth and Reality*, London: George Allen & Unwin

Glosecki, S.O. (1989) *Shamanism and Old English Poetry*, New York: Garland Publishing Inc.

Wallis, Robert J. (2003) *Shamans/Neo-Shamans: Ecstasy, Alternative Archaeologies and Contemporary Pagans*, London: Routledge.

Wilby, E. (2011) *The Visions of Isobel Gowdie: Magic, Witchcraft and Dark Shamanism in Seventeenth-Century Scotland*, Eastbourne: Sussex Academic Press

Winterbourne, A. (2007) *When The Norns Have Spoken: Time and Fate in Germanic Paganism*, Wales: Superscript.

In the story of *Ghvthisavari*, it is immortal water that brings his brother back to life, and so warrants its inclusion in this section of the book. It is at the same time, however, a tale worthy of further analysis for a number of reasons.

The reference to the apple in the second paragraph is no doubt a biblical one, from the story of Adam and Eve, despite the fact that the fruit in question is by no means certain to have been an apple in the original source. The metaphorical phrase "forbidden fruit", any object of desire whose appeal is a direct result of knowledge that cannot or should not be obtained or something that someone may want but is forbidden to have, refers to the Book of Genesis, where it is the fruit of the Tree of Knowledge of Good and Evil eaten by Adam and Eve in the Garden of Eden.

In Western Europe, the fruit was often depicted as an apple, possibly because of a misunderstanding of, or perception of intentional dual meaning in, the Latin malum, a noun that can mean evil (from the adjective malus), but also apple. In the Vulgate, Genesis 2:17 describes the tree as de ligno autem scientiae boni et mali: "but of the tree (lit. wood) of knowledge of good and evil" (mali here is the genitive of malum). The larynx in the human throat, noticeably more prominent in males, was consequently called an Adam's apple, from a notion that it was caused by the forbidden fruit sticking in Adam's throat as he swallowed.

Some Slavonic texts state that the "forbidden fruit" was actually the grape, which was later changed and made into something good, much as the serpent was changed by losing its legs and speech, and the Zohar (the text of Jewish Kabbalah) also claims the fruit was a grape.

Other Christians sometimes assert that the "forbidden fruit" was the fig, from the account of their using leaves of this tree to cover themselves (also the fig tree is the only fruit tree explicitly mentioned in the Genesis 3 context).

Because the tomato, a fruit, is in some Slavic languages called "rajčica" or "paradajz", (both words are related to paradise – "raj" means "paradise"), there are also many of the opinion that it is the forbidden fruit of Genesis. Before the seventeenth century, tomatoes were regarded as poisonous in many European countries, lending credence to the rumours of its forbidden past.

Some Rabbinic traditions regard the forbidden fruit as wheat: wheat is "khitah" in Hebrew and thus is a pun on khet, "sin". Still, many believe the quince, which pre-dates the apple and is native to Southwest Asia, was the forbidden fruit.

Other potential forbidden fruits of the Garden of Eden include the pomegranate, the carob, the etrog or citron, the pear, and, more recently, the datura. And a fresco in the 13th-century Plaincourault Abbey in France depicts Adam and Eve in the Garden of Eden, flanking a Tree of Knowledge that has the appearance of a gigantic Amanita muscaria, a poisonous and psychoactive mushroom.

In some interpretations, the 'apple' was a metaphor for sexuality, 'the first sin' and so forth. This is heavily disputed, especially since the first commandment given to Adam and Eve in the Book of Genesis was to "be fruitful and multiply." Additionally, when the first woman was presented to the first man, God said in Genesis 2:24: "That is why a man will leave his father and his mother and he must stick to his wife and they must become one flesh", thereby implying sexuality (sub voce) and parenthood (father and mother).

In any case, whatever the reason for the inclusion of the apple in the story may in fact have originally been, one thing is for certain – it adds a sense of timelessness and universality to the appeal of the tale.

Again and again in stories "...*we see how things appear in threes: how things have to happen three times, how the hero is given three wishes; how Cinderella goes to the ball three times; how the hero or the heroine is the third of three children.*" (Booker, 2004, p.229). In the story of *Ghvthisavari* it is three creatures that the hero has dealings with – the stag, wild boar, and griffin. But why does the triad, a group or series consisting of three items, feature over and over again in folktales and legends, wherever they may originate from? The answer is that it has long been of significance for a number of reasons, some of which are listed below:

- Photius, who was Patriarch of Constantinople from 858 to 867 and from 877 to 886, observed that the triad is the first odd number in energy, is the first perfect number and is a middle and analogy, and the Pythagoreans referred it to physiology, the cause of all that has the triple dimension. It was also believed to be the cause of good counsel, intelligence and knowledge, and a Mistress of Music, mistress also of Geometry, possessing authority in whatever pertains to astronomy and the nature and knowledge of the heavenly bodies, connecting and leading them into effects. Every virtue was also believed to be suspended from it, and to proceed from it. It was also known as a "Middle and Analogy," because all comparisons consist of three terms, at least; and analogies were called by the ancients "middles." Additionally, on account of the perfection of the triad, oracles were delivered from a tripod, as is related of the Oracle at Delphi.
- *Ezekiel xiv. v. 14* mentions three men who saw a creation, destruction and a restoration; Noah of the whole world, Daniel of the Jewish world Jerusalem and Job of his personal world.
- There is also the Hindu Trinity of Brahma, consisting of Brahma, Vishnu and Siva; Creator, Preserver and Changer.
- The Three Fates can be listed too – Clotho, Lachesis and Atropos. Then there are the Three Furies – Tisiphone, Alecto and Megæra. Mention can also be made of the Three Graces – Euphrosyne, Aglaia and Thalia. In

addition, there are the Three Judges of Hades – Minos, Æacus and Rhadamanthus.

- As for the Druids, their poems are noted as being composed in triads.

- Then there is the transcendent importance of the Christian Trinity. In old paintings we often see a trinity of Jesus with John and Mary. The Christian trinity of God the Father, God the Son, and God the Holy-Ghost can also be added to this list.

- For the Jews, monograms of Jehovah were triple; thus three rays and the *Shin*, and three *yods* in a triangle.

- In the *Timæus* of Plato, the Divine Triad is called *Theos:* God; Logos, the Word and Psyche, the Soul. Indeed it is impossible to study any single system of worship throughout the world, without being struck by the peculiar persistence of the triple number in regard to divinity; whether as a group of deities, a triformed or three-headed god, a Mysterious Triunity, a deity of three powers, or a family relationship of three Persons, such as the Father, Mother and Son of the Egyptians, Osiris, Isis and Horus.

- Three is a notable number in the mythology of the Norseman too: the great Ash-tree Yggdrasil supported the world. It had three roots; one extended into Asgard, the abode of the Gods; one into Jotenheim, the home of the Giants, and the third into Nifleheim, the region of the Unknown. The three Norns (Fates) attend to the root in Asgard: they were Urda (the past); Verdandi (the present) and Skulda (the future).

- The *Talmuds* are crowded with quaint conceits concerning the triad, and many are very curious:- He who three times daily repeats the 114th Psalm is sure of future happiness; Three precious gifts were given to the Jews – the Law of Moses, the Land of Israel and Paradise. In three sorts of dreams there is truth: the last dream of the morning, the dream which is also dreamed by a neighbour, and a dream twice repeated. Three things calm a man: melody, scenery and sweet scent. And three things improve a man: a fine house, a handsome wife and good furniture. Three despise their fellows: cooks, fortune-tellers and dogs. Three love their fellows: proselytes, slaves and ravens. Three persons live a life which is no life: he who lives at another man's table, he who is ruled by his wife, and he who is incapable from bodily affliction.

- Then there are three keys which God keeps to himself, and which no man can gain nor use: the key of life, the key of rain and the key of the resuscitation of the dead. *Taanith*, 2; 1 and 2; The Jewish butcher of Kosher meat must use three knives: one to slaughter the animal, another to cut it up and a third to remove the suet, which it is forbidden to eat. Three acolytes had to attend the High Priest when he went in to worship: one at his right, one at his left, and one had to hold up the gems on the train of his vestment.

- Among the Brahmins there were three great *Vedas*; three *Margas* or ways of salvation; three *Gunas*, the *Satva*, quiescence; *Rajas*, desire; and *Tamas*, decay. Three *Lokas*: *Swarga*, *Bhumi* and *Patala*; heaven, earth and hell. Three Jewels of wisdom, the *Tri-ratnas*: Buddha, *Dharma* and *Sanga*. The three Fires are the three aspects of the human soul: *Atma*, *Buddhi* and *Manas*. There were three prongs of the trident, and three eyes in the forehead of Siva. Note also the three-syllabled holy word *AUM*.

- At the Oblation of the Elements in the Celtic Church, three drops of wine and three drops of water were poured into the chalice. And in the present Christian Church we notice three crossings with water at Baptism, three Creeds, the Banns of Marriage are published three times and a Bishop in benediction makes the Sign of the Cross three times. In Roman Catholic churches, the Angelus Bell is rung three times a day, a peal of three times three for the heavenly hierarchies of angels: Pope John XXII ordered that the faithful should say three *Aves* on each occasion.

- There is also the *Threefold Law* (a.k.a. the *Law of Return*) in the *Wiccan Rede*, an ethical code for witches, which adds a reward for those who follow the code, and a punishment for those who violate it. The law states that "All good that a person does to another returns three fold in this life; harm is also returned three fold."

- Last but not least, mention should be made of the *I Ching* or *Book of Changes*, one of the oldest of the **Chinese classic texts,** as it contains a **divination** system based on triads. The standard text originated from the ancient text (AAA) transmitted by Fei Zhi (AA, c.50 BCE - CE 10) of the Han Dynasty. Each hexagram represents a description of a state or process and is composed of four three-line arrangements called *trigrams*, of which there are eight: — *khien, tui, li, chan, sien, khan, kan* and *kwan*; each expressed by figures of one long and two short lines. (Adapted from *The Triad* in Westcott, 1911, pp. 41-48).

Three is linked with the phases of the moon (waxing, full and waning), and with time (past, present and future). Pythagoras called three the perfect number in that it represented the beginning, the middle and the end, and he thus regarded it as a symbol of Deity. The importance of the number in this particular folktale could well be the result of the influence of Christianity and its use of the Trinity, but it also refers to the three stages in the cycle of life and so adds to the universality of the story's appeal.

Not only does Ghvthisavar have dealings with three different creatures, he is also able to communicate with them and understand their language – another attribute traditionally associated with shamans. Using the hair, the bristles from the wild boar and the feathers from the fledgling, or the bodily secretions of creatures is also something that commonly appears in the concoction of magical potions used for protection – not only in the Caucasus but universally. That the horns of the stag reach to heaven, and that is where the fledglings nest in the tree, are not purely coincidental either.

Another point worth mentioning is that being forbidden to eat or drink any food is commonplace and to be expected in an account of what is in effect a shamanic journey. When journeying in other realities, the eating of food is often forbidden. See, for example, Paul Radin's account of the Winnebago Indian Road to the nether world in the Thirty Eighth Annual Report, Bureau of American Ethnology, Washington, DC, 1923, pp. 143-4, which is reproduced in Berman 2007.

A shamanic journey is one that generally takes place in a trance state to the sound of a drumbeat, through dancing, or by ingesting psychoactive drugs, in which aid is sought from beings in (what are considered to be) other realities generally for healing purposes or for divination – both for individuals and/or the community. A shamanic story, such as *Ghvthisavari* can be defined as one that has either been based on or inspired by a shamanic journey, or one that contains a number of the elements typical of such a journey.

Also worthy of note is the way in which when given his brother's wife, Ghvthisavari puts a sword between them when he lies down, and does not touch her:

'Tsatloba' is a custom widely spread among the people living in the mountains of Georgia (Pshavi, Khevsureti). It usually starts with the onset of puberty (most frequently, when teenagers are 14 years old). In the past, the more 'tsatsali' a girl or boy had, the more respected she/he was. Conversely, if they did not manage to acquire a 'tsatsali', they were considered to be either not attractive or just useless.

It was believed that a teenager should attract 'tsatsali' by their behaviour. In the past, the young people involved in this custom could even be relatives but now this is not allowed. By this custom, the teenagers had a right to kiss and caress each other exclusively above the waist. If, accidentally, the girl got pregnant, both of the people were punished and they could be exiled from the community or even punished by death. If the tsatsali were not relatives, they could get married when they were old enough for that.

Naturally, this custom was based on sexual attraction. If the girl or the boy were attracted to each other sexually, they were vowed to be like brother and sister (implying that they would not get involved in proper sexual intercourse). First, the boy would go to a secluded place indicated by the girl (generally, in the woods, in a shed or a barn, far from their homes). After some time, the boy would venture to go to the girl's house at night and stay there until dawn. Doing so, he would be cautious not to be noticed by the girls' parents. On the other hand, even if he was noticed, the parents would pretend that they had not seen anything. (Adapted from Mzia Tsereteli: *Gender - Cultural and Social Construct: A course of lectures for the students of Social Studies* (Editor-in-chief Marine Chitashvili), Tbilisi 2006).

Another custom in the region of Khevsureti is that for a Georgian a guest is considered to be sent by God. Thus, guests are respected and trusted and hosts try their best to please them. In order to show how much a guest was trusted and honoured, in Khevsureti a host would ask his male guest to lie in the same bed either with his virgin daughter or, if he did not have one, the host would ask a neighbour or his children's friends with his wife. A dagger was put in the bed between the couple as a guarantee of chastity. It is also possible that the woman was also given the chance to defend herself if the guest (especially, after the feast) did not prove to be as honourable as he was expected to be.

Anyway, enough of a preamble, and time now for the tale itself:

Ghvthisavari (I am of God)

THERE was once a king, who had a daughter so beautiful, that he was in constant fear lest someone should carry her away by force and marry her. So he had a huge tower built in the sea. He shut his daughter up in this tower, with an attendant, and felt relieved.

Some time passed, when one day the attendant noticed something floating on the water. She was surprised when she saw that it was a large apple. She stretched out her dress, and the sea waves rolled in and left the apple in her skirt; she took it in her hand, and ran to her mistress. The beautiful maiden had never in her life seen such a big apple, and was very much astonished. After dinner she peeled it, gave the skin to her companion, who quickly finished it, and ate the inside herself.

In a short time they both became pregnant. The king was informed of this. On hearing the news, he pressed his head between his hands, and could not contain his wrath. He commanded one of his huntsmen, saying: "Go to the tower in the sea, take thence my daughter and her companion, and carry them to the wildest and most desert spot in my kingdom. Kill them, and bring me their hearts and livers to show me that they are dead. No one must know this story, save thee and me; if it becomes known it shall cost thee thy life."

The huntsman went to the tower, and declared the king's orders to the princess and her companion. The beautiful maiden said:

"What will it avail thee to kill us? Take us to a lonely place, and no one will know whether we are dead or alive."

The huntsman was not moved by these entreaties; he took them to a desert place, drew his dagger and was about to strike the fatal blow, but at the last moment he felt sorry for them, and gave up his intention. He caught two hares, killed them instead of the women, took out their hearts and livers, and returned with them to the king. The king believed them to be the hearts and livers of the princess and her attendant; he gave the huntsman gifts, and sent him away.

The princess and her companion were left alone in the wild wood, and they had nothing to eat and drink.

In a short time the princess brought forth a beautiful boy, and the attendant, eight tiny little dogs. The princess called her son Ghvthisavari (I am of God). He grew as much in a day as other children grow in a year; he became so handsome, brave, and strong, that everybody loved him.

Ghvthisavari used to go out hunting; he took his dogs with him, and provided game for his mother and her companion.

Once he went into a town to a smith, and asked him to make a bow and arrows. The smith made from nine litras of iron (a litra = 9 lbs.) a bow and arrows. Ghvthisavari bent it. Then the smith added more iron, and made the bow again. Ghvthisavari slung his arrows over his shoulders, his dogs followed him, and he went away. On the way he hunted, and took food home to his mother.

The next day he went to hunt again. He shot an arrow and killed a goat, he shot another, and killed a stag; he drew his bow a third time, and his arrow stuck in a devis' house. In this house there were five brothers, devis – one two-headed, one three-headed, one five-headed, one nine-headed, and one ten-headed; and their mother, who had only one head. They saw an arrow suddenly fall down and stick in the fire. They all jumped up and pulled the arrow to draw it out, but they were not able to move it. The mother helped them, but it was of no use. Then all the brothers rose up, they left their mother to watch, and set out to seek him who had shot the arrow. Ghvthisavari bethought himself, and set out he followed the flight of the arrow to see where it had fallen.

He went on and on until he came to the devis' house. He looked in and saw in the middle a fire burning, in which stuck his arrow. He went in, and was about to draw the arrow out when the devis' mother cried:

"Who art thou, wretch, who darest to venture here? Art thou not afraid that I shall eat thee?"

"Thou shalt not eat me," said Ghvthisavari, drawing out his arrow and hurling it at the old woman. He cut her into a hundred pieces, gave her to the dogs, and told them to throw her into the sea. He lay down in the devis' house and rested.

The devis wandered far and wide in their search, but nowhere could they learn any tidings of him they sought. Then they said:

"Perhaps someone will enter our house and steal, while we are here. Let one of us go home, and the rest watch here." Each wished to go, and promised to run back again as quickly as possible. But the devis chose the two-headed brother, and sent him.

The two-headed brother came, and saw that his mother was no longer there, but in her place was a strange youth. He clapped him on the shoulder, and cried out:

"Who art thou, wretch, who darest to venture here? For fear of me, bird cannot fly under heaven, nor can ant crawl on earth. Art thou not afraid that I shall eat thee?"

"Thou shalt not eat me," said Ghvthisavari, throwing an arrow. He cut him into a hundred pieces, gave him to the dogs, and made them throw him into the sea.

The four remaining devis waited for their two-headed brother, but he did not come. They thought that perhaps he was staying eating him who had shot the arrow, so they sent the three-headed brother.

The three-headed devi came home, and found neither his mother nor brother, and called out: "For fear of me bird cannot fly in air, nor can ant creep on earth. Who art thou who darest to venture here? Art thou not afraid that I shall eat thee?"

"Thou shalt not eat me," said Ghvthisavari, casting an arrow. He cut him into a hundred pieces, gave him to the dogs, and made them throw him into the sea.

The remaining brothers waited and waited, and then sent the five-headed devi. He too boasted, but Ghvthisavari did unto him that day even as he had done unto the others. Then the nine-headed devi went. The same thing befell him as his brothers.

The ten-headed devi was now the only one left. He thought to himself:

"My brothers are probably eating, and will not leave anything for me." He rose and went too.

He went in and saw that his mother and brothers were not there. Instead, there was a strange youth, lying down resting. The devi called out:

"From fear of me the bird in heaven dare not fly, on earth the ant dare not crawl. Who art thou who darest to venture here? Art thou not afraid that I shall eat thee?"

"Thou shalt not eat me," said Ghvthisavari, throwing an arrow and killing him. He drew out his sword, cut off his heads, and gave him to the dogs to throw into the sea.

Ghvthisavari was left master of the field. Then he said to himself:

"I will go and bring my mother and her companion here, and I shall live as I like." He went forth and brought them, settled them in the house, and prepared for the chase.

From the sea there staggered forth the last ten-headed devi, and hid under a tree. When Ghvthisavari had cut off his heads, in his haste he had left the tenth on. Now, it was in this head that the soul was placed, so the devi came out on to the shore, full of wrath.

The next day Ghvthisavari again went out hunting. His mother, wishing to see the surroundings, went out of the house into the garden. As she walked about, the devi suddenly appeared at the foot of a tree. The devi pleaded, saying:

"Do not give me up! Do not tell thy son that I am hidden here!" Ghvthisavari's mother promised, and when Ghvthisavari went out to the chase, his mother always took food and drink to the devi. And at last she loved him.

Once the devi said to her:

"Why should we live thus? We see each other only in secret, I am continually in terror of thy son. Go home now, lie down in bed and pretend to be ill. When thy son comes home and asks thee what is the matter, say to him: 'Go to such and such a place and bring me some pieces of stag's horns as a remedy.' When thy son goes to the stag, it will butt him with its horns, and then thou and I shall remain here alone."

The woman agreed to this plan, went in and lay down in her bed. Ghvthisavari came home, and seeing his mother sick, he said to her:

"What is the matter? Tell me what will cure thee, and I will find it, even if it be bird's milk." His mother said:

"If thou canst bring to me a piece of such and such a stag's horn, from a certain place, I shall be well; if not, I shall die." Ghvthisavari slung his bow and arrows over his shoulders, took his dogs and set out.

When he had gone some way, he came to an immense wide plain, where he saw a stag feeding. It had such large horns that they reached to heaven.

He sat down and took an arrow. Just as he was about to let it fly, the stag made a sign, and cried out:

"Ghvthisavari! Ghvthisavari! why shoot me? What have I done to deserve this of thee? Dost thou not know that thy mother has deceived thee. She seeks thy ruin, therefore has she sent thee hither. Behold, here is a piece of my horn, take it, and here is one of my hairs, take it with thee also, and when thou art in trouble, think of me, and I shall be there."

Ghvthisavari thanked the stag joyfully, and went away.

He went home with the stag's horn to his mother. She took it, and thanked him.

The next day Ghvthisavari again went to the chase. His mother immediately hastened to the devi and said:

"Ghvthisavari has returned unharmed, and has brought the stag's horn."

"Well," said the devi, "pretend to be ill as before, and tell him that he must bring a wild boar's bristle from such and such a place, else there is no cure for thee."

The woman ran in, lay down in bed, and began to moan. Ghvthisavari returned, and seeing his mother ill, he asked her:

"What is this, mother? What aileth thee? Tell me what will cure thee, and even bird's milk I will not leave unfound."

"If thou wilt seek in such and such a place, and bring me a bristle from a certain wild boar, then all will be well, but if not, I shall die."

"May thy Ghvthisavari die if he find not this!" said Ghvthisavari, slinging his bow and arrows on his shoulders, and taking his dogs, he set forth on the quest.

He went a long way, and came into a wood. There he found a boar's lair, but boar was there none. He went on a little, and saw another lair, but again there was no boar in it. He went away once more, and saw the boar itself. It had changed its lair twice, and now lay in a third. Ghvthisavari approached it, took aim with an arrow, but, as he was about to let it fly, the boar cried out:

"Ghvthisavari! Ghvthisavari! What have I done to harm thee? Why kill me? Dost thou not know that thy mother has deceived thee? She wishes for thy death, therefore has she sent thee hither. But since thou wouldst like a bristle, pull out as many as thou wishest, and take them with thee."

Ghvthisavari came up, took a bristle, and was going away, when the boar took out a hair, gave it to him, and said:

"Here is also a hair for thee; when thou art in trouble remember me, and I shall come to thee." Ghvthisavari took the hair, thanked the boar, and went away.

He came home, gave his mother the bristle, and again hastened out to the chase. His mother ran immediately to the devi, and said complainingly:

"Ghvthisavari has returned unharmed, and has brought me the boar's bristle."

The devi replied:

"Then go, again, pretend to be ill, and say to Ghvthisavari: 'If thou wilt go to a certain place, where a certain griffin (phascundzi) lives, and bring me the flesh of its young, I shall be well; if not, I shall die.' Thou knowest he cannot do that, and thou and I shall stay here together."

The woman rejoiced, ran quickly back to bed, and began to moan. Ghvthisavari came in, saw his mother in bed, and asked the cause. His mother replied as the devi had commanded. Ghvthisavari answered:

"Then may Ghvthisavari die if he find not what thou wishest." He went away.

He went on and on, and at last came to a plain, where stood a very big tree, whose top stretched to heaven. On a branch there was a nest, from which fledglings peeped out. Then, from far away in the sky, there appeared a huge, strange bird, something like an eagle. It swooped down, and just as it was about to seize the young birds, Ghvthisavari drew his bow, and killed it. Just then appeared the griffin, mother of the young ones. She thought Ghvthisavari her enemy, and was about to seize him, but her fledglings cried out that he had killed the bird that would have drunk their blood, and had saved them.

Although the griffin did not bring up more than three birds in a year, yet she was in constant terror until they had learnt to fly, because this same bird used to seize and eat them.

When she learnt that Ghvthisavari had killed their cruel enemy, she came to him, and said:

"Tell me what thou wishest? why art thou come hither? and I will immediately satisfy thy desire."

Ghvthisavari said:

"I have a mother who is ill; unless I take her young griffin's flesh she will die."

The griffin said in reply:

"Thy mother deceives thee, and is not ill at all; she seeks thy death. Here are my fledglings, if thou wantest them, but do not kill them, take them with thee alive." She pulled out a feather, and gave it to him, saying: "Take this with thee, and when thou art in trouble think of me, and I shall be there." Ghvthisavari thanked her heartily, took away a fledgling, and went home.

He came in, gave the young griffin to his mother, who said:

"Now, my child, I am quite well, and shall want nothing else," and she sent him away.

Ghvthisavari went out hunting. The woman went out hastily to the devi, and complained, saying:

"Ghvthisavari has brought the fledgling, and he himself has returned alive."

The devi was very angry, but calmed down and said:

"When Ghvthisavari comes in, tell him he must be bathed, and when he sits down in the tub, put a cover over him and call for me. I will come and hammer down the lid, and throw him into the sea." The woman rejoiced at this plan, went in and heated water. When Ghvthisavari came in, his mother said: "Come, child, I will bathe thee, it is some time since thou wert bathed." Ghvthisavari did not like this, but at last he consented. He sat down in the tub, his mother shut the lid, and called the devi. The devi ran in and hammered down the lid. Then he lifted the tub up and rolled it into the sea.

Ghvthisavari's dogs saw this; they went to the edge of the water and barked. They barked until the very stones might have been moved with pity. Then they said:

"Let us go and seek his friends, they may perchance help us." Four remained and four went to seek his friends. They came to the stag, then to the boar, and then to the griffin. These all arose and immediately went to the water's edge.

They thought and planned, and at last decided what to do. They said to the griffin:

"Fly up high, strike and cleave the water with thy wings, the tub will appear, the stag will throw it on to the shore with its horns; then the boar will strike with his tusk, the tub will break, and Ghvthisavari will come forth." They all did as they were told.

The griffin flew up high in the air, beat with its wings as hard as it could; it cleft the sea into three. The tub was seen, and the stag did not let it fall, but threw it with its horns, and let it down on the shore. Then the boar struck it, crying out:

"Ghvthisavari, lie down in the bottom!" He struck with his tusk, broke the tub, and Ghvthisavari came forth unharmed.

After this the friends went away, each to his own home. Ghvthisavari remained thinking. Just then a ragged swineherd came along. Ghvthisavari said to this swineherd:

"Come, give me thy clothes, and I will put them on."

The swineherd was afraid, and thought:

"This stranger will take my coat and not give me his," and he ran away. Ghvthisavari pursued him, took off his clothes, and put them on himself; he gave the man his coat, left with him his dogs, and went away.

He came home as if he were a beggar, and asked alms of his mother. When the devi saw him, he looked ferociously at him, and said:

"Go back to the place whence thou camest, lest I do to thee as thou deservest."

Just then Ghvthisavari saw his bow and arrow in the corner, and cried out:

"We shall see who goes hence! I am Ghvthisavari!" Saying this he drew his bow, shot first the devi and then his mother, killing them both. Then he went to the companion, scolded her well for not warning him, and killed her too. He went away, brought his dogs, and returned to the house to rest.

There came then, no one knows whence, a certain youth; he saw his father, mother, and their servant were all killed, and asked Ghvthisavari to fight. He was Ghvthisavari's mother's son by the devi; Ghvthisavari did not know this, and came to the combat. A long time they struggled, a long time they strove, but neither could strike the other. Then Ghvthisavari said:

"Come, friend, let us each tell the other his story, and afterwards we can fight."

"Good! Very well," they said, and each told his tale.

When Ghvthisavari learnt that this was his own brother, he said: "It is indeed fortunate that we told our tales first, for if we had killed each other there would have been no help for it."

After this the two brothers went into the house, and they lived happily together.

Once Ghvthisavari said to his younger brother: "Let us go, brother, and seek our fortunes, we shall become like old women if we live thus."

"I am willing," replied the younger; so they set out.

They wandered on until they came to a place where two roads met. One led to the right and one to the left. In the middle of the roads stood a stone pillar, on which was written: "Whoever goes to the left will come back, but he who goes to the right will never return." Ghvthisavari took the road to the right and his brother went to the left. Ghvthisavari said:

"Know that if the water on the roof changes into blood I shall be in trouble. Come then to my aid. If the water on my roof turns into blood, I shall come and help thee in thy trouble." Then they divided the dogs: each took four, said farewell, and set out.

Ghvthisavari went on until he came to the shore of a sea, so vast that the eye could not measure it. Twelve men were on this side, twelve on that. Whoever comes to this sea must jump over; if he leaps over without wetting his feet he may marry the king's daughter, who is very beautiful; if not, he is drowned in the sea; and whoever dares not jump at all is seized by the sentinels, and taken before the king.

Ghvthisavari came, and the sentinels told him the conditions. Ghvthisavari took a spring with all his might and main, and leaped over so that not a drop of water touched him. He saw the other sentinels, and they told him that they must take him before the king. When the king saw him he rejoiced, and gave him his fair daughter to wife.

That night Ghvthisavari asked his wife:

"Where is the best hunting to be had in the kingdom?"

She replied:

"If thou goest to the left thou wilt return; if thou goest to the right thou wilt never return." The next morning Ghvthisavari arose at daybreak, took his bow and arrow, and went to the right hand.

He shot an arrow and killed a hare, he tied its feet and left it; he shot another arrow and killed a stag, he bound its feet together and left it too. He shot a third arrow, and it stuck in a burning fire.

He went on and on until he reached this fire. Then he killed a stag, put it on the fire, and sat down at the side. He roasted meat, ate some, and gave some to his dogs. Behold, no one knows whence, a toothless old woman appeared. She begged Ghvthisavari to give her something to eat. He did so; he ate, but the old woman ate ten times more. For every mouthful Ghvthisavari took she took a basketful. Ghvthisavari looked on in amazement. The old woman finished all the food. Then she took a little stone and threw it at Ghvthisavari's bow and arrow. They turned into stone, and fell on the ground. Then she took the little stone and threw it at the dogs, who also became petrified. She took them one by one in her hand and swallowed them. Ghvthisavari was stupefied; he seized his bow and arrow to kill the old woman, but he could not move it; it fell to earth. Then the old woman turned her stone towards Ghvthisavari, who lost his strength, and became as a corpse. The old woman lifted him up in her hand and swallowed him. At that moment the water changed to blood, and the younger brother knew that Ghvthisavari had fallen into misfortune, and set out to help him.

When he had gone some way he came to the water's edge, on each side of which stood the twelve sentinels. He leaped across.

The sentinels were surprised, they thought it was Ghvthisavari, and asked him whence he came and whither he was going. The youth told them nothing, and did not let them know who he was. He came to the king. That night he was given his brother's wife, but when he lay down he put a sword between them, and did not touch her. Then he asked her:

"Where is the best hunting?"

She replied: "If thou goest to the left thou wilt return, if to the right thou wilt never return. Do not go; did I not tell thee the same thing yesterday?"

"I asked thee, and I went one way, but did not like it; now I ask thee again," said the youth. He rose the next morning, and went to the right hand.

When he had gone a little way he saw the dead hare with its feet bound; he went on further and saw the dead stag with its feet bound. He said to himself:

"My brother must have come this way; this is some of the game he has killed." He again went on, and saw the fire burning. Beside it lay Ghvthisavari's bow and arrow, and he said to himself: "Here my brother has met his fate." Then he killed some game and roasted it on the fire.

There appeared, no one knows whence, the same old woman. She sat down and waited for her share of roast meat. In eating, the old woman's behaviour was the same as before. When she had finished the food she was still hungry. She took a little stone, and lifted it to throw at the dogs. The youth thought to himself: "It must have been in this way that this old woman swallowed my brother Ghvthisavari." He seized the old woman by the throat, cleft her breast open, and took out Ghvthisavari and his dogs. Then he killed the old woman, and poured her blood over Ghvthisavari, the dogs, and the bow and arrow. Ghvthisavari and his dogs came back to life, and the bow and arrow were raised from the earth. When Ghvthisavari woke to consciousness he said:

"Ugh! I have had such a dream."

Then his brother said:

"Thou hast not dreamt," and he told him what had happened.

Ghvthisavari rejoiced, and they both went to their new kinsman, the king. On the way, Ghvthisavari was very melancholy, for he thought that his brother must have married his wife. His brother looked at him and said:

"May this arrow strike me on the part of my body that has touched thy wife, and kill me." Thus spoke Ghvthisavari's brother, and threw up an arrow. It fell, struck him in the little finger, and he died.

Ghvthisavari left his brother, went in, and, when he had learnt all, was deeply grieved. He went, no one knows where, found immortal water, and brought his brother back to life. Then he found him a fair wife, and they dwelt together, happy in fraternal affection and in love.

30:1 The expression 'bird's milk' is often used in Georgian to signify a great rarity.

Taken from *Georgian Folk Tales*, by Marjory Wardrop [1894], at www.sacred-texts.com . Published by David Nutt in the Strand, London [1894]. Scanned, proofed and formatted at sacred-texts.com, July 2006, by John Bruno Hare. This text is in the public domain in the United States because it was published prior to 1923. This story comes from a short collection of folk tales by Marjorie Wardrop, who also translated the Georgian author Rusthaveli's *The Man in the Panther's Skin*. Although many of the motifs of these stories are also found in European folklore, there are characters and plot elements which localize them in the central Asian area.

* * *

The Waters have been described as the reservoir of all the potentialities of existence because they not only precede every form but they also serve to sustain every creation. Immersion is equivalent to dissolution of form, in other words death, whereas emergence repeats the cosmogonic act of formal manifestation, in other words re-birth (see Eliade, 1952, p.151). And, following on from this, the surface of water can be defined as "the meeting place and doorway from one realm to another: from that which is revealed to that which is hidden, from conscious to unconscious" (Shaw & Francis, 2008, p.13)

A Poor Man and a Snake

There was a poor man who had nothing except his wife, a daughter and a son. He had no land, no cattle, absolutely nothing, so there was no way he could provide for his family at all. He had to send his son to be a shepherd and work for a rich neighbour, his daughter was employed looking after their home, and he and his wife worked as servants.

His wife was washing laundry, cleaning wheat, spinning wool, sewing and knitting and, as a reward for all this, all she was getting was a mart* (approximately 4 kg) of wheat. The man was cutting the grass for the rich neighbour's cattle, bringing back wood from the forest, and was ploughing this nobleman's land, and this is how they managed to survive.

One day during harvest he took his sickle and went to the field. He worked very hard but at the end of the day his owner put just two marts* of wheat for him in a sack as payment for two months' work. Nevertheless, the poor man took the sack and went home happy. When he crossed the field though, he noticed that the katchatchebi (a type of bush) were on fire, and that a snake was crawling toward its hole in the ground but would clearly be unable to make it in time, before the flames engulfed him too. So it crawled on to a bush, but then that bush caught fire too.

When the poor man approached the bush, the snake begged him for help: "Traveller, for sake of your blessed parents, save me from burning, and I will be of use to you. Help me by providing me with a stick I can crawl down."

The poor man didn't hesitate. He immediately held his stick out. The snake rolled on to it, and was saved by then wrapping itself around the poor man's neck.

"If you're giving me a reward, please give it to me now and then we can each go our separate ways," said the man.

"You are asking me for a reward? Are you crazy! I'm first going to strangle you and then to eat you," replied the snake. "But if you find someone who can tell us that they have ever met or heard about a snake being thankful, I promise I'll let you go. If you can't though, then you will surely die."

"Let someone else judge then please."

The snake agreed. They decided to listen to three opinions before making a decision. What could the poor man do? He had no choice but to accept the situation and just hope for the best. He was walking with the snake wrapped around his neck. Who knows if they were walking a little while or lot, but they saw a traveller. The poor man told him his story and asked him his opinion, or at least to teach him how to get rid of the snake.

"Well I've travelled a lot," the traveller replied, "but I have to admit I've never seen or heard any snake replying kindly to kindness. So I'm afraid I really can't help you."

"So his opinion proved to be of no help to you" said the snake. "And it looks as if I'm going to get my way after all."

Shortly afterwards they met a bear along the way, and the poor man asked him the same question.

"My ancestors and I have always been regarded as consultants by all the other animals because of our vast knowledge, but even I have never come across such a case – never in my lifetime have I heard of any snake responding with kindness to kindness. Try asking someone else," was the only answer the bear could come up with.

At this point, the poor man got so scared that his knees started to shake. But luckily he saw a lion coming towards them, and decided to tell him all about his problem.

The lion roared loudly, and this is what he said: "If you both have a complaint and want me to be the judge, then both of you should stand in front of me. As you know, judging is normally done that way. Then you can each tell me your side of the story. And I'm afraid that's only way I can pass any judgement. So you put your rucksack down on the ground and stand over there," said the lion to the man, "and you too, come down and stand next to him," he said to the snake.

So the poor man put his rucksack down and the snake slithered down on to the ground too.

The lion roared at the man once again, even more loudly this time: "Nobody should ever have mercy on those who don't value kindness and do wrong instead. So my judgement is this: Use your sword, hanging on your belt and cut the snake's head off."

On hearing this, the snake frantically tried to climb up on to the man again but the man quickly took his sword and cut the snake into two.

"Now use a stone to beat the bottom half of the snake," continued the lion "and, with the stick, throw it away as far as you can. Then bury it exactly there where it lands. The top half of the snake, with its head, will crawl to the Spring of Eternal Life, bring water back from there and, if it manages to wet its other half, the snake will grow seven times longer then it was before. So wait and watch until it comes back and make sure you crush the head with a stone, for if you don't do that, it won't die."

The head part of the snake reached the Spring of Eternal Life, just as the lion had said it would, held water in its mouth and came back to look for its bottom half, but of course it wasn't there. In anger, it started to lash out at the stones that had been used to bury it. But the man did as the lion had told him, took one of the stones and used it to crush the snake's head.

"You see, you were lucky to meet me," the lion spoke again, "otherwise what would have happened to you? You must have been crazy to think you could trust a snake!"

"Don't worry – I've learnt my lesson this time," the poor man replied, and I'm not going to be cheated by anyone ever again.

"Come with me and I will teach you where the Spring of Eternal Life is. It might make your life easier in future. But, whatever you see there, try not to be afraid."

The lion walked in front and the man followed him. They crossed the field and got to the foot of a mountain. A bare cliff rose in front of them and it blocked their way. The man was gobsmacked but the lion found a narrow entrance and squeezed in through it. The man followed his example, and they came upon the entrance to a cave. There they found a dragon seated on a nest of eggs, waiting for them to hatch.

The dragon got angry on seeing the lion and the man, and opened its enormous mouth ready to swallow them alive. But at that exact moment the lion bit its neck and dug out the dragon's eyes. The dragon tried to catch hold of them but couldn't see a thing. The man helped the lion and together they killed the dragon. They also destroyed all its eggs.

It turned out that this dragon was the guardian the Spring of Eternal Life. In the roof of the dragon's cave the lion and the poor man saw a skylight, from where water was gushing down. And this was the Spring of Eternal Life they had come in search of.

The lion and the man washed their faces in the spring; the man took some water with him too and they started the journey back home again.

When they came to a safe place, they said good-bye to each other and went in different directions from there on.

The man went home to his family with his sack. It so happened though, that at the same time, all the king's messengers were out and about, delivering the message that the king's only son had been fatally wounded, and that the king was prepared to give half of his kingdom and his eternal gratitude to anyone who could save him!

Although the poor man had barely stepped through his doorway when he heard the news, he immediately packed a small bag, took his water with him, and set off to see the king. He arrived at the king's palace on the following day. He gave the king's son water and he became seven times more handsome, seven times more powerful and also seven times healthier than he had been before.

The king was over the moon and held an enormous feast to celebrate the miraculous recovery of his beloved son. However, let's be honest. Which king gives half of his kingdom to a poor man? None! But he did give the poor man oxen and three sacks of wheat. Better than nothing.

The poor man returned home happy. He still had to work hard to provide for his family, but ever since then one thing has changed – he has never made the mistake of trusting a snake again.

* * *

The Ossetians are "the distant descendants and last representatives of the northern Iranians whom the ancients called Scythians and Sarmatians and who, at the dawn of the Middle Ages, under the name of the Alani and Roxolani, made Europe quake with fear" (Bonnefoy, 1993, p.262).

The ancestors of the Ossetians were the Alans, and the Daryal Gorge takes its name from them ("Dar-i-Alan", Gate of the Alans). They wandered as nomads over the steppes watered by the Terek, Kuban and Don Rivers until the Huns, under Attila, swept into Europe and split them into two parts. One group of the Alans moved into Western Europe; along with another wandering people, the Vandals, they passed through Spain into

North Africa, where they disappear from history (Pearce, 1954, p.12). The other group were forced southwards and eventually settled along the Terek, immediately north of the main Caucasus Range. There they entered into trading and cultural relations with other people of the Black Sea region, and in the tenth century were converted to Christianity.

Polytheism is characteristic of the world of beliefs of nomads, and the Samartian Alans were no exception to this. Batraz was the Alan god of war, and there was also a mother goddess who was the equivalent of the Greek Potnia Theron. As for the cult of the Sun and the Moon, beside altars dated from the end of the 6th and the beginning of the 5th centuries BC, smoking vessels have been found. It is highly likely that the people who took part in the rituals would have been overcome by the smoke produced from these vessels, and that this could have resulted in them entering altered states of consciousness, which is of course what shamans frequently did (see Vaday, 2002, pp.215-221).

The dissolution of the Soviet Union posed particular problems for the Ossetian people, who were divided between North Ossetia, which was part of the Russian SFSR, and South Ossetia, part of the Georgian SSR. In December 1990 the Supreme Soviet of Georgia abolished the autonomous Ossetian enclave amid the rising ethnic tensions in the region, and much of the population fled across the border to North Ossetia or Georgia proper.

So the Ossetes today are a divided people, with one group (Kudakhtsy) living in South Ossetia (Georgia) and the majority living in North Ossetia (Russia). The latter are comprised of two ethnic sub-groups, Irontsy and Digortsy, each of them possessing their own dialect. North Ossetia ... was renamed 'North Ossetia-Alania' in 1994 with an aspiration to drop 'North Ossetia' at some stage, so that remaining 'Alania' would include both the South and the North (Matveena, 1999, p.89).

However, in the summer of 2008, everything changed. For on 7 August, after a series of low-level clashes in the region, Georgia tried to retake South Ossetia by force. Russia launched a counter-attack and the Georgian troops were ousted from both South Ossetia and Abkhazia. This was followed by Russia recognizing the independence of the two breakaway regions. The rest of the world, however, has not followed suit, and what the future will bring remains uncertain at this point.

* * *

In the next story, it is the transformative power of water that ensures two young people who love each other deeply can never be separated come what may:

The Rain – A Legend of the 11th Century

At the time of Tsar George I (the rulers of Georgia were called Tsars = kings), in the 11th century, there lived the famous general, Kaiours, belonging to the glorious Orbeliani family. It is known that these princes trace their ancestry from an emperor of China and more than once intermarried with our rulers, in consequence of which their position at the court of Georgia was an exceptionally pleasant one. It is necessary to add to this that the submission and zeal of the princes Orbeliani fully repaid this distinction. They occupied from generation to generation the post of Sparapet, that is, of general in chief of all the Georgian forces, and astonished the world with their bravery. When George went to war with the Greeks, Kaiours was taken prisoner, and as this took place during the battle of Shirimna, where a great many Georgian leaders, among them the generals Ratt and Zovatt, brothers of Kaiours, were lost, the Tsar for a long time thought that Kaiours had died together with them. It was only when the negotiations for peace began, that Emperor Vassilii the Second proposed to the Tsar to exchange Kaiours for fourteen fortresses, viz., for one in Tao, one in Basiani, one in Artana, one in Kola, one in Djavaheta, in Shavhetta, and so on; and besides he demanded as hostage George's three-year-old son, the Tsarevitch-successor Bagrat.

"I am so much indebted to the princely family of the Orbelianis that I would consent to give half my kingdom for them," answered the Tsar.

At the end of the negotiations it was decided that the Tsarevitch-successor should remain as hostage at Constantinople until the Greeks had succeeded in introducing their administration in the above mentioned fortresses and in no case longer than three years. There were those who criticized the Tsar for giving away fourteen of the best fortresses in exchange for one man, but the people almost killed them. The general confidence in the warlike capacities of the princes Orbeliani was so boundless that many openly said: "Let only Kaiours come back and by him we shall not only regain possession of all our fortresses, but with the help of God we shall obtain the foreign ones!" There was no end to joy when he returned home. More than all rejoiced his twelve-year-old daughter Tamara. The captivity of the father was a great grief to her, as in his absence her mother and brother died. Seeing Tamara riding forth by herself to meet him, accompanied by an old gamdela (nurse) and several bitchos (young boys, servants), the hero Kaiours, the very glance of whom turned whole regiments to flight, cried like a child. Father and daughter tenderly embraced and for a long time could not speak.

The cries of joy among the people ceased, all remembered the good princess and the pretty boy, who had accompanied her everywhere, and sadness darkened the general joyousness. Kaiours was the first one to recover. He addressed those who had come to meet him and invited them to his house, to feast with him. "Tamara tries by her courtesy to take the place of my princess," he said, "the Lord is not without mercy; during my captivity he gave me a son in exchange for the one whom he took away. Plinii," Kaiours says, turning to a handsome youth, standing behind him, "help thy sister and me to serve the guests." All looks were now fixed on Plinii; tall, well-built, with fine, regular features, he bore an unmistakable stamp of aristocratic descent. Feeling himself the object of general interest, he blushed and dropped his eyes, like our bashful young ladies, and this modesty at once disposed everybody in his favour.

The old nobleman Alexander, whom for his bravery and warlike successes they all called "the Macedonian," sat down by Kaiours and began to speak thus: "Friend, thou hast rightly said that the Lord compensated thee for the loss of thy son by a fine youth, whose attachment and filial respect to you we all see and which dispose us in his favour, but we should also like to know who he is and why thou didst adopt him?"

"During my captivity," answered Kaiours, "the Lord sent me a friend. He was a well-known dignitary, a favourite of the Emperor and did not need the friendship of the prisoner, nevertheless not a day went by that he did not visit me. We related to each other our war reminiscences and soon began to love each other like brothers. When I received news of the death of my wife and son, his friendly sympathy was my sole consolation. He told me about his life and thus I found out that he had lost his loving companion on the day of Plinii's birth. The boy is now eighteen years old and healthy, but not strong, and must be carefully looked after. Before my departure my friend fell ill and called me to him. 'I am dying,' he said, 'and thank God that this happens before thy departure, because I am going to hand over to your care my greatest treasure. Adopt Plinii instead of that son whom God took away from thee. The doctors think that his health needs a much warmer climate than ours.' I swore to love and treat him like my son and hope that the Lord will help me to fulfil my vow!" continued Kaiours.

"Thou didst satisfy my curiosity on one point," said Alexander, "now I want to find out something else, but for this we must repair to some other place. My heart also grieves about the son, who by the will of the monarch is among the young men accompanying the Tsarevitch-heir to Greece. Although our separation will not exceed three years, yet it does seem an eternity to me." At these words the old men retired, and when they returned they were carrying bowls of horn, filled with wine. With a gay countenance they addressed the feasting crowd. "Friends," said Alexander, "congratulate me and help me to thank Kaiours, who gives me the very best he possesses: I asked the gift of the hand of his daughter for my boy." Numberless people offered their congratulations and the feasting continued far into the night. Kaiours and Alexander saw each other often, the latter always hastened to communicate any news about the son. In the meantime it was discovered that the young men who accompanied Bagrat were learning all European languages and sciences.

Kaiours thought thus: "I gave my daughter an entirely Georgian education, she knows neither European languages nor those arts by which the women over there so attract young men; would she not appear strange to your son?"

Quite unexpectedly was heard Plinii's sweet voice. "Allow me to say a word." The old men stared at him; he stood before them all red with emotion.

"Speak!" was their unanimous answer.

"My late father did not mind spending any sum for my instruction, they taught me everything that is to be learned in our country. I easily learned the sciences, and if you permit me I shall be only too glad to educate my sister, who herself has a great passion for learning."

Permission was given, and from then on the young people were inseparable. Under Plinii's direction Tamara soon acquired great perfection in Greek. They studied together the poets, committing the finest parts to memory. Tamara's wonderful voice grew still grander when she learned from Plinii how to accustom it to the rules of music. A harp was obtained, and for whole hours at a time they rejoiced in song. To the young people days, weeks, and months went by with extraordinary rapidity, they were perfectly happy and for a long time could not imagine how they had become so dear to each other. Being confident in Kaiours's affection, they fearlessly announced to him their discovery. But as Kaiours had once given his word to Alexander, he did not consider it right to break it. The lessons were stopped and Plinii forbidden to visit Tamara except in the presence of her father.

The young people's happiness suddenly turned to deep grief, which Kaiours, who loved them sincerely, secretly shared. After a few days of such torture, Plinii could not restrain his feelings and found occasion to have a secret interview with Tamara. With tears in his eyes he implored her to run away with him to Greece and there be married, but neither prayers nor tears could persuade her to become disobedient to her father.

"As thy wife should be so superior to all others as thou art the most beautiful man in the world," said Tamara, "how canst thou wish to marry a runaway girl? No, Plinii, let us wait! God is omnipotent! He knows, sees and esteems everything in due measure. He knows very well whether we find it easy not to be able to see each other, and I am sure that if we do nothing to provoke him, he himself will find means to stop our separation; only this I pray thee, do not forget me and don't try to find an occasion to see me secretly."

Morning and evening, day and night, Tamara prayed to God to make an end to their separation, and the Lord answered her prayer. Once upon a time, accompanied by an old nurse and a bitcho (young boy servant), she started on a pilgrimage to some distant monastery where there lived an old man of ascetic life. To him Tamara revealed her grief and the old man led her into his garden. There in the presence of all he began to pray for her, and suddenly a terrible cloud appeared, lightning was seen and fearful strokes of thunder were heard. Those who were present fell to the ground from fright. At last the storm was over.

"Arise!" said the prior, "the Lord has heard us sinners and

comforted Tamara!"

"But where is she?" they asked.

"There," answered the old man, pointing to a magnificent fragrant lily, which had suddenly appeared in the midst of his garden. "The Lord turned her into a flower," he continued.

The people would not believe it. The nurse spread a rumour that the crafty abbot had hidden Tamara. Forgetting godly fear and fearing Kaiours's wrath, she insulted and cursed him. The boy servants, among whom there were many Mahometans, searched the whole monastery, all the surrounding woods and bushes, and not finding Tamara anywhere, they killed the holy old man and burned down the monastery. The ancient building stood in flames, also the stone enclosure, many a hundred-year-old tree, the huge library, in fact all the scanty good of the images. Alone the church and the lily into which Tamara had been trans-formed were spared.

Upon hearing of what had occurred, Kaiours and Plinii hastened to the spot. In the church there was nobody, everything else represented a field of coal and ashes. Tamara was nowhere to be found. Only in the midst of all these ashes there grew a splendid, fresh, fragrant white lily.

Plinii was the first to approach her and began to cry. Kaiours followed him and was very much startled. He noticed that when Plinii's tears fell on the coal surrounding the lily, her tender leaves grew quite yellow from jealousy; on the other hand when they dripped into the lily she grew red from joy.

"Tamara, is it thou we see?" asked the father.

Just at that moment there came up a little breeze and Kaiours and Plinii heard distinctly as though the leaves spoke:

"It is I, father!"

The inconsolable father could not stand the loss of his daughter and immediately died from grief, but poor Plinii cried so much and so long and so fervently prayed to God that he might be united with Tamara, that in the end the Lord transformed him to rain. I have heard that in bygone times whenever a dryness set in the inhabitants of the surrounding villages hastened to the abandoned church, around which lilies always grew in abundance, and picked whole baskets of them. They scattered the fragrant harvest in the fields and gardens and the young maidens sang Tamara's song. The lovely melodious composition was as fragrant and clean as the dear flower which they glorified. This song, indeed, is Tamara's very prayer, showing all her childish faith in God's almightiness. It ends with an invocation of Plinii, who, they say, always appears in the form of a warm, beneficial rain. I heard even that these lilies preserved a rare capacity, viz., sometimes to grow red, sometimes yellow, and our maidens thus concluded that these flowers could tell one's fortune. Each maiden notices one flower and after the rain goes to look for it. Is the lily yellow, the young girl entertains great fears as to the fidelity of her lover; is it red, she never doubts his attachment to her. Whether this quaint custom still prevails I don't know. I am always sorry when some such tradition becomes forgotten! In our ancient legends there was so much of the truthful, honourable and elevated that these circumstances alone rendered them most instructive.

* * *

for Project Gutenberg (This file was produced from images generously made available by The Internet Archive/American Libraries.)

As this legend was translated into English from Russian rather than Georgian, there are several minor errors mainly in the translation of proper names and toponyms. For instance, the correct versions of the toponyms are Basiani, Artaani, Javakheti, and Shavshetti.

Tsar is a Russian word for a Georgian mepe (king); tsarevitch would be mepistsuli; Vassill I is Basil II (Emperor of Byzantium);

Giorgi I (1014 – 1027) is a monarch well-known to Georgians as he is one of the main characters in Gamsakhurdia's 'The Dexter of the Artist' as a builder of Svetitekhoveli, the main Orthodox cathedral in Georgia.

Giorgi I took advantage of the fact that the Emperor of Byzantium was occupied fighting against the Bulgarians to return Tao, one of the regions taken away by force, to Georgia. . Later, however, Basil II, the Bulgar Slayer ordered Giorgi I to leave Tao. As a result, Georgia got involved in a very difficult war which ended with Byzantium's victory. Not only did Georgia have to return Tao to Byzantium, but also Basil II took Bagrat, the heir to the throne, to Constantinople as a hostage.

Vassili the Second, also known as Basil II the Bulgar Slayer (958 – December 15, 1025) was a powerful Emperor and a talented soldier who expanded his Empire to the Balkans, Mesopotamia, Georgia, and Armenia .

Prince Bagrat, later known as Bagrat IV Kuropalati (1027 – 1072), succeeded his father Giorgi I to the throne of Georgia at the age of nine, and his reign was also a constant struggle with opponents seeking the throne and against the Byzantine emperors.

Bichi (xelis bichi) was a male servant in a household ("bichi" is a boy in Georgian), and Gamdeli (gamzrdeli) was a nurse ("gamdeli" means one who raises or looks after a baby). – M.R.

In the next tale, the loss of water from a broken water jug leads to a loss of equilibrium within the community where the event takes place, in the same way as the shortage of natural resources caused by our greed and lack of consideration for the community we are part of leads to an imbalance in the ecosystem.

Cane Woman

There was a certain king who had a son. One day the prince was playing "kochaoba" (a Georgian children's game played with sheep's ankle bones) with some other boys when a girl with a water jug passed by. The prince picked a stone, threw it at her and broke her jug.

The girl, crying, went to her mother and said: "The prince broke my water jug."

The mother replied: "Don't curse him for what he's done this first time because he's his parents' only child. Instead, take another jug, and if he breaks that one too, curse him then by uttering the following words: May you fall in love with a girl who doesn't have a human mother!"

The girl took a second jug and went out to the stream. The prince broke that jug too with another stone. So this time the girl did curse him: "May you fall in love with a girl who doesn't have a human mother!"

As soon as the prince heard the curse, he went home and fell ill. Many doctors tried to cure him but without success. One day the boy asked his father (the King) to allow him to ride a horse. The king gave him the horse and the prince left, but he never came back.

The king searched high and low for his son but couldn't find him anywhere. Then he ordered everyone in his kingdom to dress in black as a sign of mourning for his lost son.

The prince travelled a long distance until eventually he came to a tower. There he saw a woman standing in front of it and, as he was tired after his journey, he asked: "Let me be your brother and stay here overnight."

The woman replied: "A guest is sent from God, so of course you can come and stay."

The prince got down off his horse, took it to the stable and entered the house. He saw a very old man whose beard was covered with moss. He said "gamarjoba" (hello) but the old man could hardly hear him. The prince explained to the old man that he was in love with a girl who didn't have a human mother and was looking for her.

The old man said: "I've never heard anything about such a girl but you can go and see my older brother. He lives in another castle and he might know."

The next morning the prince continued his journey and, as he was riding he thought to himself that as he had difficulty in making the old men hear and understand him, with the oldest brother it was going to be even more difficult. Then he came to the third tower with a woman standing in front of it once again. "Let me be your son and stay here overnight," he asked her.

"With pleasure," the woman replied, "but first I need to tell my husband and see what he says."

The boy got down off his horse and waited. The woman entered the house and didn't come out for quite a long time because her husband was asleep and she knew he would be angry if she woke him up. Finally she put on her golden flip-flops, paced noisily up and down in them, and in that way roused him from his sleep.

"Why did you wake me up?" Her husband asked.

"We have a guest at our door and he wishes to stay with us overnight. That's why I woke you up," replied the woman. The husband allowed her to call the guest in, so the woman went out and invited the prince to enter.

The boy took his horse to the stable and entered the house. He saw her husband and, surprisingly, he looked very young. He sat down together with him and they started to talk. The prince explained to the man that he was in love with a girl who didn't have a human mother and that the purpose of his journey was to find her.

The man informed him that he had never heard anything about the woman but he knew that, near the border, three brother devis had been living for a long time, and that they had a mother who stays behind to spin wool when the brothers go hunting every morning. He also knew that the mother always faces the sun while sitting. "You have to approach her from behind, and then ask her the following question: 'Mother, I am very thirsty. Could you give me a drink?' If you do this she won't eat you and, if she won't be able to tell you what you want to know, then nobody else could." Their conversation ended there and the man told his wife they would like to eat.

"What should I prepare?" The wife asked.

"We have a pumpkin in the attic and you can cook that," the husband replied. She brought the pumpkin down from the attic but her husband didn't seem to be pleased with it. "Take that pumpkin back and bring down a second one." So the woman took the first pumpkin back to the attic but then brought the very same pumpkin down again.

The woman started to prepare the pumpkin and the two men chatted together. "Both your younger brothers look so much older than you and I could hardly make them understand me," the prince remarked. "However, I believe that you are the oldest and wonder how you manage to keep yourself looking so young."

"One of my brothers has the side of a donkey as a wife," replied the old man, "and the other one a dog's mouth, but my wife is a very special human being. You saw yourself just now that we had only one pumpkin in our attic but, because of me, she took it up and brought it down again as if we had two. If my brothers asked their wives to do the same, they would probably throw the pumpkins at their husbands and refuse to go along with such a story. To give you another example of just how special she is, when I go to sleep she doesn't even enter the house so as not to wake me up. Today was the first time when she has had to wake me up, and just now when I looked in the mirror, I saw a grey hair for the first time as a result. So you can understand now why both my brothers have grey hair and look so old, while I still look relatively young."

They had supper and went to bed. The next morning the prince continued his journey. He approached the devis' mother from behind, as he had been instructed, and asked her what he had been told to do: "Mother, I am very thirsty. Could you give me a glass of water please?"

"If you hadn't called me mother, I would have eaten you," she answered. Then she went into the house and brought him the glass of water he had asked her for. "Even ants cannot crawl on the earth and birds cannot fly because they are frightened of my sons," she continued. "So how come you were brave enough to approach us?"

"I don't care who eats me – devis' children or others," replied the prince. "My only concern is to solve the problem I am faced with." And then he told her all about the woman he was in love with. The devis' mother told him that that she had never heard anything about such a woman, but would nonetheless do what she could for him.

In the evening she hid the prince and then the three devis came home.

"We can smell a human here," they all remarked.

"No, my children," their mother replied. You have travelled a lot and you probably brought the smell of a Christian person into the house with you from the dirt on your clothes." The devis believed their mother. They then cooked and gobbled up what they had brought back with them from the hunt.

The next morning the brothers went back to the forest to hunt again. The old woman then took the prince from hiding and gave him a knife. She instructed him to go to the forest too, to cut down three trees and bring them to her.

The prince did as he was told, but the tree trunks were so heavy that it was a real struggle for him and his horse to bring them back. The old woman had no trouble lifting them at all though. She placed the three trunks over her knees and broke them as if they were just thin sticks.

"These three are unfortunately not the kind I was hoping for," she remarked. So the old woman then went to forest herself and brought three different tree trunks back with her.

"Get on your horse and follow me," she then said to the prince.

The woman picked up the three trunks with no effort at all, and then ran so fast that the boy found it very difficult to keep up with her, even on horseback. Soon they approached the sea. The boy dismounted, the woman gave him a knife and a whetstone, and told him to sharpen the knife on it so that it could cut through the trunks if she needed to use it. The boy started to sharpen the knife but after a while he got frightened, thinking that she was going to use the knife to cut his head off. The woman noticed that his hands were shaking and asked him what the problem was, so he told her of his fears: "I'm frightened that you might be planning to kill me."

"I'm not going to kill you," she answered, "And of that you can be certain. I could have done if I'd wanted to, but you said mother to me and that saved you."

So the boy sharpened the knife, and then the woman hurled all three trunks into the sea and shouted something as she did so. At this point, the waters parted, and three cane trees emerged.

"Now run quickly, cut these trees down, and bring them to me before rain starts," the old woman instructed the boy.

The boy did as he was told, cut the trees down and brought them back to the shore. He just made it back in time before a big wave hit from behind, nearly knocking him over with its force. Then the woman cut off the top of the trees and started to pray. While she was praying, one of the trees split into two and the most incredibly beautiful girl came out of it. They took the girl home with them. When they reached the old woman's home, she baked a loaf of bread, gave the young couple a horse, a jug of water, and this is what she said to them: "Go home now, the pair of you, and never get off the horse until you reach your front door."

They followed the old woman's instructions and rode until their home was in view, but by then the boy was confident enough to do what he felt like: "This is already my father's kingdom and I already feel I'm at home, so let's dismount from the horse and have a rest now."

The girl reminded him of what the old woman had said, but the boy persuaded her to do as he suggested. They left the horse to graze, went down to the river, and found a suitable spot in the shade there. The boy laid his head on the girl's lap and fell fast asleep. An Arab woman, as black as the night, came to them, and started talking to the girl: "Let's go and have a swim in the river together." Cane Woman refused at first because her husband was sleeping on her lap, but the Arab woman managed to persuade her, and they put a saddle under the head of the king's son's head instead. The Arab woman had a swim first and then she said: "You swim now and I'll keep guard so that nobody comes and watches you." So Cane Woman took her clothes off. At this point, the Arab woman pushed her into the water and then cast a spell over her: "May you become a fish!" And a fish is what Cane Woman turned into.

The Arab woman got dressed in Cane Woman's clothes, removed the saddle from the king's son's head and put his head on her own lap instead. When the boy woke up and looked at her, he was shocked. "What on earth has happened to you? How did you get so dark?" he asked.

"Don't you remember? We were warned by the old woman not to dismount from the horse, but you made me do so, and that must be the reason why I turned so dark." The Arab woman replied.

And so they continued on their journey until they came to the king's palace. The king, on one hand, was very happy to see his son and he ordered his subjects not to wear black any more. On the other hand he was rather upset, and he told his son so: "Can this really be the woman you went to so much trouble for?"

"I can't do anything about it now, however disappointed you may be," was his son's answer. "She must have been my fate." And so they were wedded.

Now while all this was going on, after many miles of swimming, the fish that had been Cane Woman came to the part of the river where the shepherds used to take the king's cattle to drink. But the cattle were frightened of the strange fish, and couldn't drink any water however hard the shepherd's tried to persuade them to, so died of thirst. The king was then informed of what had taken place.

It was actually forbidden to fish in that part of the river, but this time the King sent all his fishermen to catch the fish. And although the fishermen caught loads and loads of fish, they could not catch the one who had been responsible for the death of the cattle.

When all the fishermen had tried and failed, one lame fisherman decided to try his luck once again. "I'll cast the net one last time before I give up" he said. This time he caught the fish and took it personally to the king.

Upon discovering the fish had been caught, the Arab woman issued orders for it to be boiled, eaten, and for all the bones to then be burnt in a fire. Everyone ate the fish and threw the bones into the fire, just as they had been told to do, but one drunken man then arrived on the scene and asked if he could have some of the fish too. "Yes, you can. But if you find any piece of bone, you need to burn it in the fire like everyone else has done," was what he was told. He was so very drunk though, that he forgot all about what he was supposed to do and threw the bone into a cattle shed instead.

The fish was eaten, the cattle were housed in the shed, and all the diners went home. Next morning everyone saw an enormous tree had grown in front of the shed and the cattle were too frightened to come out. This was because the tree shook violently and made a roaring sound whenever they tried to do so.

This time the Arab woman issued orders for a lime kiln to be built, for the tree to be cut down and then chopped up into tiny pieces, and for every single wood chip from the tree to be burnt in the kiln.

Everyone did as they were told. They built the kiln and began to cut the tree down. At that point, someone new arrived, and this is what he said: "An axe was made for me today and I would like to try it out to see if it works or not." The tree cutters were pleased with his offer. While the man was testing his axe, a single wood chip flew from his blade and disappeared into the air, without anyone noticing the occurrence. The tree was then cut down, chopped up and burned completely, except for that one single chip.

That chip ended up in the middle of the road in another kingdom. One day everyone in that kingdom went to a shrine to pray. And there was one old woman among all these people. On her way back home she started to collect sticks for her fire and found the wooden chip in the middle of the road. "I'm not going to burn this," she said to herself, "but will use it as a lid for a pot."

Each time the old woman used to go out, Cane Woman turned back into human form again. Then she would sweep the floor, clean the house from top to bottom, and prepare food for the old woman, before turning back into a wood chip again in time for her return. "When we lived together you didn't listen to a word I said," the old woman complained to daughters-in-law. "So I don't understand why, when we no longer live together, you apparently love me so much now that you clean my house every day and make me dinners too."

And this was their reply: "There is an old saying that we have separated from fire but not friendship. When we were living together we were quarrelling all the time, but now that we are not, we must do our best to love each other instead."

The old woman decided to find out for herself which daughter-in-law was helping her, so she pretended to go out but actually stayed inside. The wood chip turned into a woman, swept the floor, cleaned the house, and threw the rubbish out, but all without leaving the house in case anyone noticed her. The old woman caught her in the act though. Cane Woman was very frightened and said to her: "Please don't kill me – I'm a Christian, just like you".

The old woman asked her who she was and where she came from, so Cane Woman told her story and explained she was the wood chip that covered the pot. The old woman didn't believe her at first, so Cane Woman turned back into the wood chip again to convince her she was telling the truth. Then the wood chip turned back into her human form again and they started to talk. "From today you are my mother and I am your daughter," is what Cane Woman said, and so they lived happily together.

One day, Cane Woman asked her mother if they had anything they could sell in the market. "Yes, my daughter," was her reply. "We have a chicken, but only one."

"Dear mother, take that chicken to the market, sell it and with the money buy me silk thread instead."

So the old woman sold the chicken in the market and got 5 shauri (old Georgian money) for it. Then she bought silk thread for Cane Woman, which cost 4 shauri, which meant only 1 shauri was left. Cane woman used the silk thread to make a carpet, and then asked the old woman to take it to the market to sell, and to buy her 2 shauri worth of silk thread this time with the money.

In the market three generals started haggling over the price of the carpet with her:

"How much is it?" One general asked

"You know the price of carpets," was the old woman's reply.

"I'll give you a hundred for it," that general said.

The old woman thought that he was taking the mickey out of her though, as the carpet wasn't worth any more than 2 manats at the most.

"I'll give you two hundred," the second general countered, but she thought that he was making fun of her too.

"Stop teasing me," was her response. "Just give me what it is worth – no more, no less."

At this point, the third general stepped in and gave her three hundred for it, and she was absolutely delighted. She couldn't wait to tell Cane Woman the good news and ran all the way home.

"I'm not sure what happened to those people when they saw your carpet," the old woman said to her daughter when she got home.

"Mother you just don't know the true value of that carpet. Even if you had asked for a thousand, they would have given that money to you."

She knitted many more of the same type of carpet and sold those in the market too. And with the money she earned they built many palaces. Then she knitted a saddle bag, embroidered with an invitation to the king's son: "This is an invitation to the whole of your kingdom to come and visit us."

She put her picture in the saddle bag and then said this to her mother. "You need to do me a favour and go to a certain kingdom. Sometimes you will need to walk, sometimes to travel on horseback. Please don't refuse to do this for me."

"I would go anywhere for you," was the old woman's reply, even to the end of the world."

"That is why I know I can entrust you with this task. Now you need to deliver this saddle bag personally to the king's son." Cane Woman added, "And if someone offers to do it for you, you mustn't let them. On no account must you give it to anyone."

The old woman took the saddle bag and left, and Cane woman gave her all the money she would need for the trip. The woman walked, then travelled on horseback, and eventually reached the kingdom Cane Woman had told her about. There she found the Arab woman, as black as the night, waiting for her.

"Where are you going?" The Arab woman asked.

"I'm going to see the King's son to give him something," was her reply.

"I'll take it to him for you."

But the old woman refused to give it to her. This made the Arab woman so angry that she hit her on the back of her head, an extremely painful blow that still hurts her today. Nevertheless, she kept her promise, delivered the invitation to the king's son personally, and he replied that he would be coming at a certain time and that they needed to get ready for him.

When the old woman returned home, Cane Woman asked her what had happened, and this is what she told her: "When I gave the saddle bag to the king's son, the Arab woman hit me so hard on the back of my head that is still hurts even now. But here is the letter he wrote to you in reply to your invitation."

Cane Woman read the letter and started to prepare for his visit. She made a wonderful supper and when the guests came she was dressed as a man. Everyone enjoyed the feast, and the king's son and the Arab woman sat together at the table. Cane Woman was the tamada (the toastmaster), and this is what she said to all the people present: "I'm sorry but I'm not feeling well. I need to leave you but will call my sister to take my place, who is a much better tamada then me anyway."

She left the room, changed out of the men's clothes she had been wearing, put on a dress, and then come out to the people and started to make toasts. When everyone got tired of eating and drinking she said: "For the evening's entertainment, I'd like to invite everyone present to tell their life story now."

Everyone said they wanted to hear her story first and she agreed, but asked two men to stand on guard by the door so nobody would be able to leave the room until she had finished. Cane Woman told them her story from the beginning. When she mentioned the Arab woman, not surprisingly she tried to leave the room, but the people didn't let her. Their response was to tie the Arab woman to the tail of her horse and it dragged her through the streets until she died. Then the King's son explained to his father that Cane Woman was the one he truly loved: "This is the woman I was going to marry but I didn't realize what had happened to her at the time."

Cane Woman and the King's son wedded and lived happily ever after.

There are many versions of the final story in this section, from various parts of the world, but in all cases it is the transformative power of water that plays the major part in the tale:

Two Losses

DURING a great storm at sea, a learned man heard the skipper giving his orders, but could not understand a word. When the danger was past, he asked the skipper in what language he had spoken. The sailor replied: "In my mother tongue, of course!" The scholar expressed his regret that a man should have wasted half his life without learning to speak grammatically and intelligibly. A few hours later the storm arose again, and this time the ship sprang a leak and began to founder. Then the captain went to the scholar and asked if he could swim. The man of books replied that he had never learned. "I am sorry, sir, for you will lose your whole life. The ship will go to the bottom in a minute, and my crew and I shall swim ashore. You would have done well if you had spent a little of your time in learning to swim."

Taken from *Georgian Folk Tales* by Marjory Wardrop [1894]. Wardrop also translated the Georgian author Rusthaveli's *The Man in the Panther's Skin*. Although many of the motifs of these stories are also found in European folklore, there are characters and plot elements which localize them in the central Asian area.

References

Berman, M. (2010) *Shamanic Journeys through the Caucasus*, Hampshire: O Books (for the background information on Ossetia).

Bonnefoy, Y. (comp.) (1993). *American, African and Old European Mythologies*. Chicago and London, The University of Chicago Press.

Eliade, M. (1991) *Images and Symbols*, New Jersey: Princeton

University Press (The original edition is copyright Librairie Gallimard 1952).

Gray, W. D. (1973). *The Use of Fungi as Food and in Food Processing*, Part 2. CRC Press. p. 182.

Matveena, A. (1999). *The North Caucasus: Russia's Fragile Borderland*. London: The Royal Institute of International Affairs.

Old Testament, Genesis 2:16-17, "And the Lord God commanded the man, saying, Of every tree of the garden thou mayest freely eat: But of the tree of the knowledge of good and evil, thou shalt not eat of it: for in the day that thou eatest thereof thou shalt surely die."

Old Testament, Genesis 1:28, "And God blessed them, and God said unto them, Be fruitful, and multiply."

Pearce, B. (1954). "The Ossetians In History." In Rothstein, A. (Ed.) (1954), *A People Reborn: The Story of North Ossetia*, 12-17. London: Lawrence & Wishart.

Radin, P. (1923) *The Winnebago Tribe*, in Thirty-eighth Annual Report, Bureau of American Ethnology, Washington, D.C.

Vaday, A. (2002). "The World of Beliefs of the Sarmatians." A Nograd Megyei Muzeumok Evkonyve XXVI.

The Zohar: The First Ever Unabridged English Translation, with Commentary (Rabbi Michael Berg, ed., Vol. 2, pp.388-390

Appendix (i): Saint George and the Dragon

In Georgian folklore, the opposition between water (chaos) and earth (cosmos) is considered on the plane of the opposition between the dragon and the ox. The dragon personifies water and the ox personifies earth (Kiknadze, *Georgian Folklore*, 2008), and no book on the subject of the four elements related to Georgia would be complete without reference to the story of Saint George and the Dragon, so here is a brief synopsis.

The episode of Saint George and the Dragon appended to the hagiography of Saint George was Eastern in origin, [1] brought back with the Crusaders and retold with the courtly appurtenances belonging to the genre of Romance. The earliest known depictions of the motif are from tenth- or eleventh-century Cappadocia[2] and eleventh-century Georgia;[3] previously, in the iconography of Eastern Orthodoxy, George had been depicted as a soldier since at least the seventh century. The earliest known surviving narrative of the dragon episode is an eleventh-century Georgian text.[4]

The dragon motif was first combined with the already standardized Passio Georgii in Vincent of Beauvais' encyclopaedic Speculum Historiale, and then Jacobus de Voragine's Golden Legend (ca 1260) guaranteed its popularity in the later Middle Ages as a literary and pictorial subject.[5] The legend gradually became part of the Christian traditions relating to Saint George and was used in many festivals thereafter.[6]

According to the Golden Legend the narrative episode of Saint George and the Dragon took place in a place he called "Silene," in Libya; the Golden Legend is the first to place this legend in Libya as a sufficiently exotic locale, where a dragon might be imagined. In the tenth-century Georgian narrative, the place is the fictional city of Lasia, and it is the godless Emperor who is Selinus.[7]

The town had a pond, as large as a lake, where a plague-bearing dragon dwelled that envenomed all the countryside. To appease the dragon, the people of Silene used to feed it two sheep every day, and when the sheep failed, they fed it their children, chosen by lottery. It happened that the lot fell on the king's daughter, who is in some versions of the story called Sabra. [8] The king, distraught with grief, told the people they could have all his gold and silver and half of his kingdom if his daughter were spared; the people refused. The daughter was sent out to the lake, decked out as a bride, to be fed to the dragon.

Saint George by chance rode past the lake. The princess, trembling, sought to send him away, but George vowed to remain. The dragon reared out of the lake while they were conversing. Saint George fortified himself with the Sign of the Cross, [9] charged it on horseback with his lance and gave it a grievous wound. Then he called to the princess to throw him her girdle, and he put it around the dragon's neck. When she did so, the dragon followed the girl like a meek beast on a leash.

She and Saint George led the dragon back to the city of Silene, where it terrified the people at its approach. But Saint George called out to them, saying that if they consented to become Christians and be baptized, he would slay the dragon before them. The king and the people of Silene converted to Christianity, George slew the dragon, and the body was carted out of the city on four ox-carts. "Fifteen thousand men baptized, without women and children." On the site where the dragon died, the king built a church to the Blessed Virgin Mary and Saint George, and from its altar a spring arose whose waters cured all disease.[10]

The figure of the dragon-slayer figures in the founding myth of Delphi, where Apollo slays the drakon Pytho, and has ancient Near Eastern roots as old as Mesopotamian Labbu. A dragon is also the enemy figure in Revelation and in the saintly legend of Margaret the Virgin.

The region had long venerated other religious figures. These historians deem it likely that certain elements of their ancient worship could have passed to their Christian successors. Notable among these ancient deities was Sabazios, the Sky Father of the Phrygians and known as Sabazius to the Romans. This god was traditionally depicted riding on horseback.

The iconic image of St. George on horseback trampling the serpent-dragon beneath him is considered to be similar to these pre-Christian representations of Sabazios, the mounted god of Phrygia and Thrace.

According to Christopher Booker it is more likely, however, that the "George and the Dragon" story is a medieval adaptation of the ancient Greek myth of Perseus and Andromeda – evidence for which can be seen in the similarity of events and locale in both stories.[11] In this connection, the Perseus and Andromeda myth was known throughout the Middle Ages from the influence of Ovid. In imagery, other Greek myths also played a role. "Medieval artists used the Greco-Roman image of Bellerophon and the Chimaera as the template for representations of Saint George and the Dragon."[12]

These myths in turn may derive from an earlier Hittite myth concerning the battle between the Storm God Tarhun and the dragon Illuyankas. Such stories also have counterparts in other Indo-European mythologies: the slaying of the serpent Vritra by

Indra in Vedic religion, the battle between Thor and Jörmungandr in the Norse story of Ragnarok, the Greek account of the defeat of the Titan Typhon by Zeus.[13]

Parallels also exist outside of Indo-European mythology, for example the Babylonian myths of Marduk slaying the dragon Tiamat.[14] The book of Job 41:21 speaks of a creature whose "breath kindleth coals, and a flame goeth out of his mouth."[15]

Others trace the origin of Saint George and the Dragon to Palestine, where the supposed dragon was controlled by Satan. The creature blocked the city's water supply and would only move if given a virgin sacrifice. Over time, all of the virgins were sacrificed except for the noble's daughter, and even she was sent to quench the castle's thirst. However, Saint George (or Mar Jiryis) arrived at the last moment on his white horse, striking down the dragon with a spear between its eyes.[16]

Notes

1. Robertson, The Medieval Saints' Lives (pp 51-52) suggested that the dragon motif was transferred to the George legend from that of his father fellow soldier saint, Saint Theodore Tiro. The Roman Catholic writer Alban Butler (Lives of the Saints) was at pains to credit the motif as a late addition: "It should be noted, however, that the story of the dragon, though given so much prominence, was a later accretion, of which we have no sure traces before the twelfth century. This puts out of court the attempts made by many folklorists to present St. George as no more than a christianized survival of pagan mythology."

2. Walter 2003:128, noted by British Museum Russian Icon "The Miracle of St George and the Dragon / Black George".

3. Christopher Walter, The Warrior Saints in Byzantine Art and Tradition 2003:141, notes the earliest datable image, at Pavnisi, Georgia (1154-58)

4. Patriarchal Library, Jerusalem, codex 2, according to Christopher Walter, The Warrior Saints in Byzantine Art and Tradition 2003:140; Walter quotes the text at length, from a Russian translation.

5. Margaret Aston, Faith and Fire Continuum Publishing, 1993 ISBN 1-85285-073-6 page 272

6, Christian Roy, 2005, Traditional Festivals ISBN 978-1-57607-089-5 page 408; Dorothy Spicer, Festivals of Western Europe, (BiblioBazaar), 2008 ISBN 1-4375-2015-4, page 67

7. Quoted in Walter 2003:141.

8. http://www.mainlesson.com/display.php?author=langm &book=saints&story=patron

9. In the earliest, Georgian version where the dragon is more clearly a representation of paganism, or at least of infernal power, the sign of the Cross itself was sufficient to defeat the dragon.

10. Thus Jacobus de Voragine, in William Caxton's translation (On-line text).
11. Booker, Christopher (2004). The Seven Basic Plots. Continuum. pp. 25–26. ISBN 978-0-8264-5209-2.
12. Theoi Greek Mythology.
13. Mallory, J. P. (1989). In Search of the Indo-Europeans. Thames and Hudson. ISBN 0-500-27616-1.
14. Combat of Marduk and Tiamat in the Babylonian Creation Myths, Fourth Tablet at Sacred-texts.com The killing of Tiamat is featured from line 93
15. Job 41;21
16. http://www.pitt.edu/~dash/stgeorge.html

Appendix (ii): To the Glory of Saint George [and Merrie England!]

THE WESTERN half of our history is closing true to form – a history that originated in myth and resulted in the loftiest reality. It began in the romantic fable of Perseus and Andromeda, and it ends on the shore of the Western Ocean to the glory of Saint George and Merrie England!

The connecting lineage and record are clear. The Hero family has been a prolific one, and widely spread, with a history full of noble diversity, but its temper has held true, and its mission of the rescue of maidens in peril, or, more largely, of distressed and wrong-headed peoples, has never been neglected: its career is a continuous picture of the ideal of the West-knightly valour in service, the duty of the strong to aid the weak. From Persia to Italy, from cultured Greece to the barbarous shore of the Atlantic, the tale of noble deeds was told, the fame of one and another brave soul was celebrated, and so Chivalry was born of Romance, and the Renaissance arose to rejuvenate a benighted old world.

Whether or not the names we read were ever or never those of actual men; whether or not anything like a dragon ever threatened forlorn princesses or devastated a smiling countryside, is of no consequence. As history – and its record may be as unsubstantial as the quickly dissolving clouds that reflected a rosy light upon the towers of a mythical Ilium – doubtless it is, for the most part, only an immortal legend repeating itself as do human generations, but it portrays, century after century, the highest virtue in the manly soul.

It is needless to spend time over the variants in what we may style the Perseus legend as written in classic and mediaeval books and poems. Stories identical in substance with that of the rescue of Andromeda from the jaws of a monster were widely related in antiquity and have not yet been forgotten. They form a class by themselves, differentiated from the traditions and fables that have heretofore been related, by the fact that always a young virgin, usually of royal birth, is delivered from impending death by a bold and ardent youth; and that in most cases there is the attendant, but less important, fact that the hero is nearly robbed of his just reward (the maiden's hand and heart) by the evil machinations of a rival who never quite succeeds. A typical example is found in far Arabia. One day, as we are told, a dragon comes to a city in Yemen and demands a beautiful virgin. The lot falls on the king's daughter, but a young knight kills the monster, and the brave adventurer gets the girl. Another very old example is that attached to the most precious relic in the storied island of Rhodes. Luke the Evangelist, the islanders say, desired to move the body of John the Baptist from its burial-place in Caesarea to Antioch, but was able to transfer only the saint's right hand, with which Jesus had been baptized. "Subsequently it was deposited in the new Hagia Sophia at Constantinople, and after further adventures reached security in Rhodes. While it yet remained in Antioch a dragon haunted the country about that city, and the people appeased the monster yearly with the sacrifice of one of their number, chosen by lot. At last the lot fell on a maid whose father greatly venerated the holy relic. Making as though he would kiss the hand, he bit off a fragment from the thumb: and when his daughter was led out to sacrifice he cast this fragment into the dragon's jaws and the monster quickly choked and perished."

A widely familiar 'St. George' legend is that belonging to Mansfield, in Germany, over whose church-door is a statue commemorating the incident. The great man of the place at the time was Count Mansfield, and near the town is a hill still called Lindberg because in former days it was the abode of a lindwurm, or dragon, to which the townspeople were obliged to give a young woman every day. Soon no more maidens were to be found except the knight's own daughter. Whereupon Count Mansfield rode forth and slew the beast, and the citizens made him a 'saint' and gave him (or somebody else!) a statue, in spite of his previous indifference as to the fate of their daughters. Mansfield is one of the many places believed locally to be the site of the famous combat of that 'St. George' whose exploits were as numerous and widespread as were those of Hercules – in each case probably a misplaced tradition of some dimly remembered fight between local barons or bullies.

A still closer approximation to the Perseus type was taken down a few years ago from the lips of an illiterate peasant woman of the Val d'Arno, Italy, and is quoted by Hartland. A part of it describes the hero finding in a seaside chapel a lovely maiden, who urges him to hasten on his way lest he suffer the fate to which she is doomed, namely, to be eaten by a seven-headed dragon. Instead of obeying her he dismounts, attacks the dragon on its rising from the sea, and cuts out its seven tongues which he carries away – these trophies proving his claim, a few months later, to the credit of the feat and the hand of the willing girl.

This seven-headed, seven-tongued hydra-dragon of fiction appears all down the ages, at least since the days of Hercules. Such a brute, to which a king's daughter is to be offered, figures in Grimm's tale of The Two Brothers, and variants may be found in folk-legends everywhere in Europe. That within comparatively recent times it was popularly believed to be a reality is shown by serious accounts of its doings in books regarded as sensible and authoritative. Conrad Gesner gives a picture in his Historia Animalium of a hydra in the form of a serpent, "the heads like those of lions and as it were ornamented with crowns, two feet in the front of the body, the tail twisted inwards." He relates that this hideous, aquatic creature was brought from Turkey to Venice in the year 1530, exposed to public view, and afterward sent to the king of France. The Italian compiler

Aldrovandus, a contemporary, illustrates in his book about serpents a seven-headed dragon; and in the Encyclopaedia Londonensis, issued in 1755, may be seen a large coloured plate of a dreadful, seven-headed creature credited to Seba, an author who published a Thesaurus of natural history about 1750, with an extensive account of it.

And so at last we come to our own Saint George! Who was this patron of the valorous, this model of devotion to an ideal of duty, this indomitable George? Nobody knows. He has been relegated to the sun-myths, and declared a mere relic of Mithraism. Gibbon and others identified him with the author of Arianism, but Eastern churches were named for the martyr before that prelate existed. It has also been said that he was that nameless Christian who tore down the edict of persecution in Nicomedia. These and other identifications have been discarded. The nearest approach to probability that any distinct personality is at the root of this heroic development of a noble idealism lies in a tradition that a Christian man named George (or its equivalent) was martyred in Palestine before the era of Constantine the Great; that he became the object of a religious cult (said to be referred to in an inscription dated A.D. 367); and that in 1868 his sepulchre was discovered at Lydda (or Diospolis) near Jerusalem, where his martyrdom is alleged to have occurred. Tradition has expanded these facts (if they be facts) into a story in many varying versions, the most acceptable summary of which appears to be the following:

"According to legend [this Christian George] was born, about A.D. 285, of noble parents in Cappadocia, eastern Anatolia. As he grew to manhood he became a soldier; his courage in battle soon won him promotion, and he was attached to the personal staff of the emperor Diocletian. When this ruler decided to enter on his campaign of persecution, George resigned his commission and bitterly complained to the emperor. He was immediately arrested, and when promises failed to make him change his mind he was tortured with great cruelty. . . . At last he was taken to the outskirts of the city and beheaded [April 23, A.D. 303] . . . . The earliest narrative of his martyrdom known to us is full of the most extravagant marvels: three times George is put to death, chopped into small pieces, buried deep in the earth, and consumed by fire, but each time he is resuscitated by God. Besides this we have dead men brought to life to be baptized, wholesale conversions, including that of the 'Empress Alexandra,' armies and idols destroyed simultaneously, beams of timber suddenly bursting into leaf, and finally milk flowing instead of blood from the martyr's severed head."

This and several other more or less extravagant, and equally, legendary accounts derived from old manuscripts and books, are related and discussed extensively in Mrs. Cornelia S. Hulst's admirable history of this essentially mythical saint or hero, and his veneration in Europe.

This was a remarkable man, whoever and whatever he was, and it is not surprising that, probably stimulated by some shining circumstance unknown to us, he became so distinguished in the religious world of his time. Besides St. Stephen, he is the only martyr venerated by the entire Church; is one of the fourteen 'great martyrs' and 'trophy-bearers' of the Greek Church, and is honoured by special masses and ceremonies in the Latin, Syrian, and Coptic communions. All over the Orient, in Greece, Italy and Sicily, many churches were dedicated to him in the sixth century, and since. His relics are scattered over the entire Church, Santo Georgio in Velabro, at Rome, possessing the head. Holweck catalogues this saint's ecclesiastical distinctions thus: "S. George is principal patron of England, Catalaunia (Spain), Liguria (Italy), Aragon, Georgia, Modena, Farrara (24 April), of the isle of Syros, dioceses of Wilna, Limburg, Regio de Calabria, and other dioceses, also of the Teutonic Knights, minor patron of Portugal, Lithuania, Constantinople. He is protector of soldiers, archers, knights, saddlers, sword-cutlers, and of horses, against fever, etc. He is mentioned daily in the Greek mass." Moslems, in fact, reverence Saint George, identifying him with the Prophet Elijah, and have long allowed Christians to celebrate a mass once a year at the tomb of the martyr at Lydda, in Palestine, now a mosque; and the first church dedicated to St. George (at Zarava, in Hauran, A.D. 514) was a re-consecrated mosque.

That the fame of this martyr had spread in very early times to Britain is shown by references to him in the writings of the Venerable Bede and in other chronicles. Ashmole says, in his history of the Order of the Garter, that King Arthur placed a picture of St. George on his banners, and Selden states that he was regarded as the patron-saint of England in Saxon times. It was not, however, until after the great Third Crusade, in which the English played the leading part, led by their magnificent prince, Richard the Lion-hearted, that George, as warrior rather than as martyr, became noticeable in that national dignity. It was believed among the disheartened crusaders before Acre that St. George had appeared to Richard in a vision and had encouraged him to continue the long and dreadful siege; and afterward the story spread that the troops themselves had beheld him, on a white horse, fighting for them above their heads in the drifting smoke of battle, as did the angel who was "captain of the hosts of the Lord" when Joshua was battling against the walls of Jericho. Even the French soldiers under Robert, son of William the Conqueror, accepted him as their patron and defender.

It is perhaps to this figure that Dr. Hanauer refers in relating this bit of folklore current in Palestine. A fountain (Gihon?) in the outskirts of Jerusalem was formerly a part of the water-supply of the city, but a big dragon took possession of it and demanded a youth or maid every time anyone came for water; until at last, as usual, only the king's daughter was left. When she was about to be sent, Mar Jirys appeared in golden panoply mounted on a white steed, and riding full tilt at the dragon, he pierced it dead between the eyes. This is probably the same spring which is noted for its intermittent flow, which the people explain by saying that the dragon drinks the water low whenever it wakes, and when the beast sleeps the water rises. The Tyrolese speak of a dragon that "eats its way out of the rock" when the intermittent spring at Bella, in Krains, begins to flow. The Maltese also have a dragon's spring which issues from a cavern with noises said to be the snorts of the monster within its source.

The returning crusaders, reporting this supernatural assistance in full faith, made a very deep impression on the credulous populace of England, who at once proclaimed this White Knight military protector of the kingdom; and in 1222 the Council of Oxford ordained that the feast day of St. George (April 23) should be observed as a minor holy day in the English Church. In 1330 he was formally adopted as the patron-saint of the Order of the Garter just then instituted by Edward III, which was equivalent to an ascription for the whole country, and he became that indeed when the Royal Chapel at Windsor was dedicated to him in 1348. He was invoked by Henry V at Agincourt (1415), where the English swept forward to victory with the inspiring battle-cry of his name.

Saint George he was for England,
Saint Denis was for France,
rings out the old song!

Thus this hero of the Middle Ages became in England more than elsewhere the favourite of the people and the principal figure of the time in mystic plays, mummeries, and religious dramas and processions, especially on Corpus Christi Day. Until recent times one of the diversions in Wiltshire and other English counties was the play "St. George and Turkey-Snipe" (a corruption of Turkish Knight), wherein a Christian knight overcomes a Saracen. The opening words of this pious drama are quoted by Miss Urlin as follows:

> I am King George, the noble champion bold,
> And with my trusty sword I won ten thousand pounds in
> gold.
> It was I that fought the fiery Dragon, and brought him to the
> Slaughter,— and by these means I won the king of Egypt's
> daughter.

It is not surprising that mistakes and legends early began to cluster around this notable character all over the continent.

Legends are the weeds of history. They are sown by winds of gossip, and bear fruits of the imagination which sometimes are sweet and wholesome but are more often ugly and baneful. They take deep root and flourish prodigiously, overshadowing the less interesting growths of fact and voucher, and obscuring, by a sort of protective mimicry, the truths in tradition. For example: where, if anywhere, among the many places, do the red flowers growing year by year on this and that meadow or hilltop, indicate the true spot "where the Dragon was killed"? Here and there we may say – as at Coventry – that is the field of the battle of so-and-so, a thousand years ago; but to get proof of it we must search among the roots of hardy fictions as botanists do for stifled native plants among the weeds of an abandoned field.

The eminent French antiquarian, Louis F.A. Maury, points out that many local dragon stories probably originated in or have been kept alive by mistaken interpretations by the unlearned of relics, pictures, and votive offerings in churches – the last-named including specimens of skeletons or bones of serpents, whales and so forth, stuffed crocodiles, big fishes and other strange animals, deposited by persons who had escaped perils by one or another exotic beast. Formerly, at least, there hung in the church of Mont St. Michel pieces of armour which the peasantry held in awe as that worn by the angel Michael when he drove that old serpent, the Devil, out of heaven. At Milan, where now stands the ancient church of St. Denis, was previously a profound cavern, in which, we are told, once dwelt a dragon, always hungry, whose breath caused speedy death to any person receiving it. The Milanese hero, Viscount Uberto, killed it, according to a local legend – the basis of which is a figure, named Givre, of a heraldic dragon on the armour of an early viscount of that city. Count Aymer, of Asti, in Savoy, owes his high place in the list of dragon-slayers, says Maury, to a heraldic dragon carved at the foot of his effigy on his monumental tomb at St. Spire de Corbil. The identification of Gozon with the myth of the destruction of the dragon of Rhodes, was owing to the accidental presence near Gozon's tomb of a commonplace picture of St. George in his famous act.

How a name may serve as a punning-peg on which to hang a courtier's story or a minstrel's ballad, which later may become an element in dubious history, is shown in a saga of King Regnor Lodbrog, a famous pirate chief of the Viking era, who, when a young man, about the year 800, showed his mettle in an exploit of gallantry of which his companions loved to sing when the drinks went round. A Swedish prince had a beautiful daughter whom he entrusted (probably when he was sailing away on some freebooting expedition) to the care of one of his officers in a strong castle. This officer fell in love with his ward, and seizing the castle, defied the world to take her away from him. Upon this the father proclaimed abroad that whoever would conquer the ravisher and rescue the lady might have her in marriage. Of all the bold fellows who undertook the adventure Regnor alone achieved success and obtained the prize. Now, it happened that the name of the faithless guardian was Orme, which in Icelandic means 'serpent'; wherefore the first minstrel who seized upon the incident to glorify the valour and renown of his prince (and retrieve the lady's reputation?) represented the girl as detained in the castle by a dreadful dragon!

It is a striking fact that, although dragons and dragon-killers were commonplaces of both ancient and mediaeval storymaking (someone has wittily said that the dragon itself was brought into being merely as a much-needed device to exhibit the valour of more or less fictitious knights) the association of this fearsome beast with George the venerated martyr-saint, is a comparatively modern addition to his history. The oldest written account of him, that by Pasicrates, does not mention a dragon. "The Greek Church, which was naturally the first to render St. George honour," as Mrs. Hulst points out, "from very early times represented him with a dragon under his feet and a crowned virgin at his side, a symbolical way of saying that he overcame Sin, for the dragon represents the Devil . . . and the crowned maiden represents the Church."

This religious feeling characterized legends of such a combat found in Greek and Russian verses, and tales of a somewhat later period, but nowhere is this worshipful hero of the Church represented as fighting on horseback. The first account of a combat between St. George and a dragon that reached western Europe was in the thirteenth century in the Latin of The Golden Legend, where a distinctly romantic flavour tinctured the holy narrative. This epic poem became popular and spread the heroic legend, which was recited in many versions, used in dramatic representations, and led to the localizing of the adventure in many different places. Where and when this poem originated remains a mystery.

In the early part of the fifteenth century The Golden Legend was paraphrased by Lydgate and introduced to a few scholarly English readers in a manuscript preserved in the Bodleian Library in Oxford. It was more widely spread by Caxton, the publisher, in the translation made by him and printed in 1483. His second edition was illustrated by woodcuts borrowed from a Dutch edition of the tale, and these publications not only informed England as to the tale brought from the East, but settled the version which has been the adopted faith of our British forefathers ever since. The crabbed old English and print of Caxton's book (William Morris issued a delightful facsimile from the Kelmscott Press) are so difficult to read now that many modern renderings in both verse and prose have been produced, of which I have chosen the authentic one by Baring-Gould given below.

And so, finally, we have come to the legend of the proper, most eminent Saint George, and his most celebrated and distinguished of all dragons – possessions peculiarly our own as Englishmen and by inheritance; and here is the creed of it for your worshipful instruction:

George, then a tribune in the Roman army, while travelling, came to Silene, a town in Libya, near which was a pond inhabited by a loathsome monster that had many times driven back an armed host sent to destroy it. It even approached the walls of the city, and with the exhalations of its breath poisoned all who came near. To prevent such visits it was given every day two sheep to satisfy its voracity. This continued until the flocks of the region were exhausted. Then the citizens held counsel and decreed that each day a man and a beast should be supplied, and at the last they had to give up their sons and daughters – none were exempted. The lot fell finally on the king's only daughter; and those who tell the story describe with vivid rhetoric the heartrending struggle of the royal father to submit to the decree, and his final victory in favour of duty to his people over his affection. So, dressed in her best, and nerved by high resolve, the princess leaves the city alone and walks toward the lake.

George, who opportunely met her on the way and saw her weeping, asked the cause of her tears. "Good youth," she exclaimed, "quickly mount your horse and fly less you perish with me." He asked her to explain the reason for so dire a prediction; and she had hardly ceased telling him when the monster lifted its head above the surface of the dark water, and the maiden, all trembling, cried again – "Fly! fly! Sir knight." His only answer was the sign of the Cross. Then he advanced to meet the horrible fiend, recommending himself to God; and brandishing his lance he transfixed the beast and cast it to the ground. Turning to the princess he bade her pass her girdle about the creature's prostrate body and to fear nothing. When this had been done the monster followed her like a docile hound. When they together had led it into the town the people fled before them, but George recalled them, bidding them put aside their fear, for the Lord had sent him to deliver them from their danger. Then the king and all his people, twenty thousand men with all their women and children, were baptized, and George smote off the head of the dragon.

Somehow, centuries ago, the people of Britain came to believe that this happened in England at Coventry; and it is no wonder that they learned and sang a Paean of victory over it, comparing George's superlative bravery with the great deeds of bygone heroes. You may find it in Bishop Percy's Reliques, and one stanza will give you the spirit of it:

> Baris conquered Ascapart, and after slew the boare,
> And then he crossed the seas beyond to combat with the Moore.
> Sir Isenbras and Eglamore, they were knights most bold,
> And good Sir John Mandeville of travel much hath told.
> There were many English knights that Pagans did convert,
> But St. George, St. George, pluckt out the Dragon's heart!
> St. George he was for England; St. Dennis was for France,
> Sing: Honi soit qui mal y pense!

I have traced the dragon in time from the birth of light out of darkness to the present, and in space from the Garden of Eden eastward to farthest Cathay, and westward to the crags that withstand the Atlantic's fury. I go out where I came in: There is no dragon – there never was a dragon; but wherever in the West there appeared to be one there was always a St. George.

* * *

Taken from *Dragons and Dragon Lore* by Ernest Ingersoll [1928] New York: Payson & Clarke Ltd. Formatted at sacred-texts.com, June 2004, by John Bruno Hare. This text is in the public domain in the US because its copyright was not renewed in a timely fashion at the US copyright office.

Appendix (iii): El Khudur [Eliyahu ha Navi, Mar Jiryis, and the Dragon]

ONE of the saints oftenest invoked in Palestine is the mysterious El Khudr or Evergreen One. He is said to have been successful in discovering the Fountain of Youth, which is situated somewhere near the confluence of the two seas [The Mediterranean and the Red Sea]. This fountain had been vainly sought for by other adventurers, including the famous Dhu'lkarneyn, the two-horned Alexander, who with his companions came to the banks of the stream that flowed from it, and actually washed the salt fish which they had brought with them as provision in its waters, and yet, though the said fish came to life again and escaped them, failed to realize the happiness within their reach. They went on their way till they came to the place where the sun sets in a pool of black mud, and their leader built eighteen cities, each of which he called Alexandria, after himself; but neither he nor his companions became immortal, because they failed to see and use the one opportunity of a lifetime.

El Khudr, more fortunate or more observant, not only found the fountain, but drank of its waters, so he never dies, but reappears from time to time as a sort of avatar, to set right the more monstrous forms of wrong and protect the upright. He is identified with Phinehas, the son of Eleazar, with Elijah the prophet, and with St George. Jewish mothers, when danger threatens their children, invoke him as "Eliyahu ha Navi," Christian as "Mar Jiryis," and Moslem as "El Khudr"; and his numerous shrines in different parts of the land are visited in pilgrimage by adherents of all three religions.

...The story of St George and the Dragon is, of course, well known in Palestine. The saint's tomb is shown in the crypt of the old Crusaders' Church at Lydda [the tomb is half in the present Christian church and half in the adjoining mosque]; and at Beyrût the very well into which he cast the slain monster, and the place where he washed his hands when this dirty work was done. The following is, briefly, the tale generally told by the Christians:

"There was once a great city that depended for its water-supply upon a fountain without the walls. A great dragon, possessed and moved by Satan himself, took possession of the fountain and refused to allow water to be taken unless, whenever people came to the spring, a youth or maiden was given to him to devour. The people tried again and again to destroy the monster; but though the flower of the city cheerfully went forth against it, its breath was so pestilential that they used to drop down dead before they came within bowshot.

The terrorized inhabitants were thus obliged to sacrifice their offspring, or die of thirst; till at last all the youth of the place had perished except the king's daughter. So great was the distress of their subjects for want of water that her heart-broken parents could no longer withhold her, and amid the tears of the populace she went out towards the spring, where the dragon lay awaiting her. But just as the noisome monster was going to leap on her, Mar Jiryis appeared, in golden panoply, upon a fine white steed, and spear in hand. Riding full tilt at the dragon, he struck it fair between the eyes and laid it dead. The king, out of gratitude for this unlooked-for succour, gave Mar Jiryis his daughter and half of his kingdom."

As already remarked, Elijah frequently appears in Jewish legends as the Protector of Israel, always ready to instruct, to comfort, or to heal – sometimes condescending to cure so slight a complaint as a toothache, at others going so far as to bear false witness in order to deliver Rabbis from danger and difficulty.

The modern Jewish inhabitants of Palestine devoutly believe in his intervention in times of difficulty. Thus, among the Spanish Jewish synagogues at Jerusalem, there is shown a little subterranean chamber, called the "Synagogue of Elijah the prophet," from the following story:

One Sabbath, some four centuries ago, when there were only a very few Jews in the city, there were not men enough to form a "minyan" or legal congregational quorum. It was found impossible to get together more than nine, ten being the minimum number needed. It was therefore announced that the customary service could not be held, and those present were about to depart, when suddenly a reverend-looking old man appeared, donned his "talith" or prayer-shawl, and took his place among them. When the service was over, "the First in Zion," as the chief Rabbi of the Jewish community at Jerusalem is entitled, on leaving the place of worship, looked for the stranger, intending to ask him to the Sabbath meal, but he could nowhere be found. It was thought this mysterious stranger could have been no other than the famous Tishbite.

Taken from *Folk-lore of the Holy Land: Moslem, Christian, and Jewish* by J. E. Hanauer. London: Duckworth & Co. 3 Henrietta Street, W.C. [1907]. Scanned, proofed and formatted at sacred-texts.com, July 2006, by John Bruno Hare. This text is in the public domain in the United States because it was published prior to 1923.

In conclusion, it should be pointed out before it is assumed that this dragon myth only dates back to the times referred to in this Appendix, that

Almost all peoples and all ages have had their dragon stories. In Greece, especially, these tales, involving both gods and heroes, were legion. There was hardly a Greek hero who did not slay his dragon, although Heracles and Perseus are perhaps the best known dragon-killers. With the rise of Christianity, the heroic feat was transferred to the saints; witness the story of "St. George and the Dragon" and its numerous and ubiquitous parallels. The names are different and the details vary from story to story and from place to place. But that at least some of the incidents go back to a more original and central source, is more than likely. And since the dragon-slaying theme was an important motif in the Sumerian mythology of the third millennium B. C., it is not unreasonable to assume that many a thread in the texture of the Greek and early Christian dragon tales winds back to Sumerian sources.

And for a detailed analysis of these sources, the book the above quotation was taken from is recommended, available online at www.sacred-texts.com

Sumerian Mythology: A Study of Spiritual and Literary Achievement in the Third Millennium B.C. by Samuel Noah Kramer, Revised Edition. University of Pennsylvania Press [1944, revised 1961]. Scanned at sacred-texts.com, October 2004. John Bruno Hare, redactor. This text is in the public domain in the US because it was not renewed in a timely fashion at the US Copyright Office as required by law at the time. These files can be used for any non-commercial purpose, provided this notice of attribution is left intact.

Moon Books, invites you to begin or deepen your encounter
with Paganism, in all its rich, creative, flourishing forms.